ALSO BY

DAVID STAHLER JR.

DOPPELGANGER

A GATHERING OF SHADES

TRUESIGHT

DAVID STAHLER JR.

An Imprint of HarperCollins *Publishers*

Eos is an imprint of HarperCollins Publishers.

Library of Congress Cataloging-in-Publication Data
Stahler, David.
    The seer / by David Stahler Jr. — 1st ed.
        p.   cm.
    Sequel to : Truesight.
    ISBN-10: 0-06-052288-7 (trade bdg.)
    ISBN-13: 978-0-06-052288-9 (trade bdg.)
    ISBN-10: 0-06-052289-5 (lib. bdg.)
    ISBN-13: 978-0-06-052289-6 (lib. bdg.)
    Summary: Raised in a futuristic frontier world colony where blindness is
the genetically engineered hallmark of every citizen, thirteen-year-old Jacob
is stricken with sight and must find his way to the city of the Seers, where
he hopes to reconnect with a girl from his past.
    [1. Blind—Fiction. 2. People with disabilities—Fiction. 3. Science fic-
tion.] I. Title.
PZ7.S78246See 2007   2006020124
[Fic]—dc22   CIP
                                                                              AC

Typography by R. Hult
1 2 3 4 5 6 7 8 9 10
❖
First Edition

To my son,
Julian

CHAPTER ONE

The great ringed moon had come and gone, moving across the sky with a speed one could almost trace if the eyes were patient enough to follow. And now even its sister moon, small and pink, tagging slowly along behind, had begun its sinking, and as the morning light crept back into the world, Jacob Manford stirred within his damp pocket of grass and dreamed.

He had been following her too long—for what seemed like hours, maybe even days—along the streets of Harmony, moving from tier to tier, from north to south, east to west, cutting through the heart of the colony each time, then twisting along unfamiliar lanes before coming back around. At first he kept losing her. She kept fading around the corners and he, running to catch up, seemed to just miss her each time. Maybe he waited, maybe he turned back—it didn't matter, she always reappeared. That was at first. Now she no longer vanished and he knew that he was gaining, that it was only a matter of time. He was close now, close enough to hear her breathing, almost close enough to touch the dark strands of hair that floated behind her though there was no breeze. He was close enough that he knew he only had to whisper her name and she would hear him.

1

"Delaney," he called, "please stop. I'm tired."

He thought she might have laughed. Or maybe it was the sound of chimes, for as he looked ahead he could see the council house before them. He picked up the pace as they climbed the ramp toward the opening set into the hill, the gaping darkness of the portal framed by the great chimes that now clamored in alarm at his approach. He had been there only once before, to be judged in the shadows of the chamber, and he knew he had to stop her. He could only imagine what they would do to her.

"Stop, Delaney. You can't go in there!" he hissed.

She must not have heard him above the clanging of the chimes, for she plunged into the gloom, spreading out her arms as if to touch the edges of the doorway before being swallowed up. He raced to the opening, then paused, reaching out a hand toward the dark only to see his fingers disappear as they breached the inky surface of the entryway. He yanked his hand back and hesitated on the threshold. He had to go in after her. The chimes ceased and still he wavered. What was he waiting for?

I wouldn't go in there if I were you, he heard a voice say. He snapped his eyes up to where a striped cat reclined above the doorway, its bulk still stretched along the ledge as it had been the morning that the listeners hauled him inside before the council. Then it had greeted him with a moment of understanding, but he felt no sympathy from it now as it peered down at him through slitted, yellow eyes. *You remember what happened last time, don't you?* its voice sounded in his mind. *Maybe this time you don't come out.*

"How can I leave her in there?" he replied. "I *have* to go get her!"

2

Suit yourself. But don't say I didn't warn you. The cat yawned, its tongue curling between needle teeth, and then stretched back against the shelf to resume its endless nap.

He shook his head, angry at the creature's indifference, and reached for the darkness again. This time his hand went deeper. Something grabbed him and began drawing him in. He gasped at the fiery touch. Try as he might, he couldn't pull away. He could only feel a burning spreading through his arm as it disappeared inch by inch, as his face came closer and closer to the opaque surface. The last thing he heard before being swallowed up was the cat's voice, a distant echo of disdain:

Foolish boy, why did you return?

Then he was falling. It was only a moment, but long enough in the silent void to feel as if he were slipping away from life. He had no sensation, only an impression of absence, and in that moment he was sure that he was blind again, this time for good. *It's all been for nothing*, he thought. But soon a mild jolt of impact shook him, and he discovered he was back on his feet and running.

There was no council chamber, no council. He was in a tunnel now instead. He could see her before him once more, very close, the thin shadow of a girl, her hair flowing back, brushing the tips of his reaching fingers. There was a strange glow before her, illuminating her profile, lighting up the rough-hewn walls of the tunnel around them. He called out to her again, trying not to cough as smoke began trailing behind her.

"Stop, Delaney! Don't run! You don't need to!" he called out, trying to wipe the tears from his blinking eyes as the smoke thickened.

3

She seemed to hear his cry, for suddenly she slowed, then halted before him in the tunnel. He slowed too and came up behind her. He reached out, put his hand on her shoulder and turned her around, desperate to see her face. He had never seen her face before.

He recoiled, blinking not from smoke now but from the erupting brightness as she turned toward him. He squinted, unable to see her face, only the twin sparks of brilliance that shone from the sockets of what were once her eyes.

"What's happened to you?" he gasped, moving closer in spite of his horror.

The light dimmed slightly, but she didn't answer as a plume of smoke rose from each eye, thick black smoke that curled up and then down, winding around his legs, fixing him in place. He could barely make out any part of her face, but her mouth seemed to curl into a smile as her eyes brightened again, growing more intense every second. He peered even closer and saw how the eyes were flickering, little tendrils of light that curled out and around her face. They were flames.

A scream sounded in his ears; he couldn't tell if it was hers or his own. All he knew was that this was the end. The cat had been right—he should never have come back. . . .

Jacob bolted upright, awakened by the sound of his own scream, for a moment not sure if he was still screaming or hearing just the memory of it. But it was quiet now. He fell back into the grass with a sigh of relief and, looking straight up, wiped away the sweat that had gathered on his forehead. The blades rose above him on all sides, forming a tunnel of vegetation, a portal through which the sky looked small and contained, its emptiness marred by only a single cloud. It was

4

a beautiful morning, clear and crisp. He told himself that the nightmare wasn't real, but it only helped a little. For the second night in a row he'd had the same dream. It was so vivid— the desperation, the fear, even the physical sensations. The sounds, the smells, the images—more real than any dream he'd ever had.

Unlike the last three days, he didn't immediately rise to his feet and continue the westward march. Instead, he lay there motionless but for his breathing, trying to let go of the memory of his dream, reluctant to shed the thin blanket that wrapped him within his nest of grass. He knew rising would reveal the stiffness he had felt yesterday when he woke soaked with dew under the same clear sky. He was tired— tired of walking, tired of thinking, his only tasks the last three days. Though he had walked late into darkness last night, before collapsing in the grass, he knew what he would see upon standing: the same uniform swell of the plains, the hills rising and falling, the grassland swaying to the currents of the breeze in waves that rippled over the terrain. He would climb to the top of one rise, only to see the same dip of little valleys that led to the next hillock, and the next.

Not that Jacob hadn't seen anything unusual. Two days ago he had seen trees for the first time—real trees, not the shrubs or small fruit trees that grew in Harmony. It was nearing sunset. Clearing a ridge, he glimpsed in a meadow a cluster of tall, dark shapes, which loomed larger as he approached, until they towered above him. With relief he discovered they surrounded a small spring-fed pool. Exhausted and thirsty, he collapsed at the edge of the spring, where the roots of the trees stretched into the water like bony fingers. Though the sun no longer blazed, it felt good to sit under the canopy of branches, to have something between himself and the sky.

There was something else he saw. As he leaned over the water to drink, a face met his, drawing nearer as he bent closer to the surface. He started at the sight before realizing it was his own face that stared back at him. It was the first time he had seen himself clearly, and he lingered over the reflection, marveling at his appearance. At the age of thirteen, his face revealed an interesting mixture of his parents' features. The overall structure—especially the cleft chin and chiseled nose—reminded him of his father, but the pale coloring of the skin and eyes was definitely his mother's. The eyes returned his stare, as if he were the reflection and the face in the pool were the real person. For a long time Jacob examined the stranger, their eyes linked until his cupped hand broke the surface, dissolving the connection into a blur of concentric circles, and he drank. He slept that night under the trees amid the roots, lulled to sleep by the rustling of the leaves.

That was the last night he'd slept with any amount of peace, free from the dream that felt like waking life. Pulling himself up now, he stretched the stiffness from his joints. He could feel hunger in his stomach, a hollow pain. For a moment, he considered looking into his canvas bag for something to eat—perhaps he'd missed some morsel of cheese, a last slice of bread. But he knew there was no point in pretending. All that remained was a single can of pears buried at the bottom of his bag. Throughout yesterday's march he told himself he wouldn't eat them, swore an oath not to. When they were gone, he'd have nothing left. It made him mad to think about how carelessly he'd packed. Why hadn't he grabbed more food? Partly it was because he hadn't been that hungry, and partly because there wasn't much left to take. Besides, he had been in a rush, so rattled by the sudden decision to leave that it never occurred to him how far he might have to go. Still, he was better off now. Wasn't he?

He turned back to the east, eyeing his dim trail running through the grass. Had it really only been four days since he had left Harmony, left his people, left the only life he'd ever known? For some reason it seemed much longer. And yet only a month ago he was still one of them. All of them were blind, content to live in the darkness, unaware of what was happening around them, oblivious to each others' actions, from minor indiscretions to the larger crimes that cut at the very heart of what Harmony was supposed to be about: purity, unity, and freedom through blindness. Oblivious, too, to the beauty and wonder of the world around them. They named their way of life Truesight, a philosophy that called for a rejection of the shallowness and deception of appearances.

Jacob glanced up at the sky where a handful of birds circled and danced in the air above him, just as they had done in Harmony. He shook his head and smiled grimly. Through some accident of fate he still didn't understand, he had discovered that Truesight itself was a deception, that it blinded his people to the realities of life, both good and bad.

They could never accept him for his difference, had tried to take his sight from him, perhaps even his life. Jacob shuddered, remembering the veiled threat Delaney's father, the high councilor, had made just before he tore himself away: *Let's just hope the surgery goes well, Jacob. The ghostbox makes mistakes from time to time.*

He didn't bother to spread his blanket out to dry in the

sun, as he had the last three mornings, but rolled the damp cloth into a bundle and shoved it into his knapsack. He needed to move; it was the only way to overcome the doubts beginning to collect in the back of his mind. He had to keep going. There was nothing else to do.

There was, however, one daily ritual Jacob kept. Pulling the finder from his pack, he extended the small device before him. Just a few weeks ago, just days before his thirteenth birthday, still blind, he'd held the cool cylinder in school for the first time and learned how to hone in on his classmate's sounder. Everyone in Harmony wore a sounder, a device that helped them navigate the settlement and identified each of them by giving off a unique pitch. Jacob had discovered his classmate in the hallway and, taking her by the hand, had brought her back to the classroom. It was barely an hour later—as he and his best friend, Egan, practiced with the finders in the schoolyard—that he experienced the first headache, the first wave of pain, the first in a series of changes that eventually brought him here to this spot in the middle of nowhere. Never would he have imagined that day that he would be using a finder in this place, for this reason.

He pressed the button and held his breath a moment before whispering her name.

"Delaney Corrow," he said.

Like always, his pulse quickened as the familiar beep began its rhythm. It only took him a moment to hone in on the direction of its greatest intensity. By now he could navigate almost completely by the location of the sun, but he loved to hear that repeating note. It was the sound of hope.

Turning the finder off, he replaced it securely in its spot. He shouldered his pack and plunged westward through the grass.

CHAPTER TWO

Wiping the sweat from the back of his neck, Jacob gazed up at the sun, now past its zenith. It was a hot day, the hottest he could remember in a long time. Though hunger still gnawed at him, satisfying it was no longer his most pressing need. All he could think about now was the thirst that had been growing in him all day. He had forgotten to bring a bottle of any kind for water, and he'd been depending on streams and springs along the way. They were few and far between. The last time he'd come across one was yesterday afternoon—a small brook, hardly more than a trickle along the bottom of a valley. Who knew when he'd find another?

He stood at the crest of a hill, gazing westward. It looked the same in all directions, just swell after swell of grass. It was about a mile to the next rise, a wide ridge taller than any he'd seen so far, so high he could see nothing behind it. He groaned at the thought of climbing it. A familiar feeling rose within him—a sickness in his stomach, a mild sensation of dizziness—but it wasn't hunger or thirst. It was fear. It was that same feeling of panic that had been rising all day, every time he thought about his situation, every time he imagined himself collapsing in the grass, swallowed up forever with no one to know where he lay. He had felt this kind of panic several times back in Harmony at the Gatherings—first as one of the crowd not long before his sight had begun to manifest itself, and then at the end when he'd stood before his people, a pariah. Now he was alone, and the feeling was more intense than ever.

As he tried swallowing, his tongue thick and swollen in his dry mouth, he wondered again if he'd made a mistake by leaving. It was his fault, after all, that they were going to blind him again and wipe his memory of sight. If he hadn't told them in the first place, he would still be living among them, living as one of them, and they would be none the wiser. They were already living a life of deception; how would his have been any worse?

None of that mattered, he realized. He couldn't change what had happened, neither would they allow him to return.

But that didn't mean he couldn't go back. He could return in secret and live among them, take food and clothing as he needed, remain in plain sight before all of them, and they would never know. He could even watch over them, like a guardian spirit, helping them when they got in trouble. He had done it before, hadn't he? Hadn't he saved that injured grower, Mitchell, from bleeding to death in the field? He had spent a whole week wandering the colony unseen. He could do it again.

Turning back, he took a couple of steps east along the slim path of trampled grass, and then stopped.

It might not be that easy. There might be one who could detect him. An image of the high councilor's face leering at him in the yellow glow of the ghostbox flashed to mind. But it wasn't just the face, it was the wink—that instant of recognition that passed between them when Jacob discovered the man could see. The whole first day after leaving Harmony, Jacob had gone over those few seconds in his mind. At first it seemed so definite, carved into a crystal moment of revulsion, but the more he recalled it from memory, the less clear it became. Now he wasn't even sure. Maybe it had been just an involuntary gesture—a twitch of the eye—or perhaps both eyes had blinked as even blind eyes do, and in the shadows he had seen only the one. In the terror of the moment, he could have imagined the whole thing.

Either way, he could risk it. Whether the man could see or not, Jacob could avoid him altogether. He never wanted to see that face again anyway.

Once more, he started numbly eastward, back the way he'd come. All he wanted was to stop the grumbling heave of his stomach, the burning in his throat. All he wanted was to live.

He had gone only a dozen steps when a sound behind him made him pause. He turned to listen.

At first it was no more than a hum, hardly distinguishable from the rustling of his legs against the grass, a single pitch like the ringing of a distant sounder. Then it grew deeper, louder, taking on an almost angry, guttural tone, a growling that peaked as a strange object flew over a ridge to Jacob's right, carried by its speed into the air, floating for a moment before dropping back down to earth, bouncing several times as it hurtled through the grass.

It was a craft of some sort. The only thing he could compare it to was the harvesters back in Harmony, the steel creatures that moved up and down rows of crops, working with the growers to process the colony's food. But this was no harvester—it moved too fast, faster than Jacob could imagine

11

anything moving. As it came closer, he could see it was taller, too, with huge, studded tires instead of revolving tracks like the harvesters had. Bars came up over the front and rear seats like a cage, and the back half of the vehicle consisted of a boxed-in storage area. Most startling of all was the sight of a man seated within the dark frame.

For a moment Jacob watched in awe as it tore down the valley, racing in his general direction. He started to raise his hands, then hesitated. This was a Seer, his first one. All the warnings, the diatribes, the sordid stories he'd heard his entire childhood came flooding back to mind. Who knew what this person might do to him, a boy, alone on the plain with no one else around? Jacob was about to take cover in the tall grass, when it occurred to him that he too was a Seer. He was one of them. Why hide?

He stood as tall as he could, waving his arms back and forth in an effort to catch the driver's attention, but the craft continued to speed along without any change in direction. It was angled to pass about fifty yards below him. He started to run down the hill in an effort to intersect it, still waving his arms. *He has to see me now*, Jacob thought, as the vehicle came closer, but still it roared along without slowing or turning in his direction.

He was only twenty yards away when it passed him. He watched it go by with a mix of confusion and disappointment—his one chance of being saved seemed to be slipping away. Then there was a piercing squeal as the craft slammed on its brakes, skidding across the grass to a halt thirty yards ahead. Jacob began running toward it, then hesitated as it started to back up toward him, slowly at first, then faster, its engine growling in reverse. He expected it to slow down as it came closer, but it kept accelerating straight at him. He dove out of the way to avoid being run over.

Tumbling through the grass, he rolled several times before landing facedown. When he picked himself up, the craft was facing him no more than ten yards away, its engine idling. A man stared at him from the cockpit, his face blank, his eyes obscured by a pair of dark goggles. At least a minute passed while the man sat unmoving, leaving Jacob with a growing sense of uneasiness.

Finally, the engine died and there was a slight hiss as the driver's side door opened. The man emerged and jumped down to the ground, holding a dark metal stick of some kind in one hand. It was about a yard long, wide at one end, narrow at the other, with a few knobs and other strange pieces protruding from the middle section. The man closed the door and turned, making no movement toward Jacob.

They stood for a moment in silence, studying each other. The man was older, perhaps his father's age, with skin nearly as tan as the growers' back home. He had an intent, angular face, and his dark hair was cropped short. His clothes were unlike the plain, blousy smocks and tunics Jacob was used to seeing. These were more tight-fitting and of different shades, with dark pants tucked into black boots, and a light shirt and darker vest. A wide belt circled his waist, lined with tiny compartments and strange-looking tools.

The man took a few steps toward him, raised his goggles with one hand and lowered the metal stick with the other.

As he came closer, Jacob noticed his eyes. They were even paler than Jacob's, though maybe it just seemed that way in contrast to the darkness of the man's skin. Jacob tried to get a sense of who this stranger was. In Harmony he had quickly

13

learned how to read people's faces. Since they didn't know anyone was watching, his blind neighbors had made no effort to conceal their expressions. But this man could see, and his face seemed guarded, steady in its control. His eyes didn't seem unkind. On the other hand, they weren't too inviting either. That was the trouble—they didn't seem like anything, though their neutrality suggested a certain sort of wisdom. Jacob had a sudden feeling that those eyes had seen a lot.

I guess I should say something, he thought.

"You almost hit me," Jacob offered as a joke. In spite of trying to sound confident, his voice came out small and thin.

"I wouldn't have," the man replied. His voice, like his face, seemed neither hostile nor welcoming, just sure. He pushed past Jacob, donned his goggles, and scanned the southern horizon, reaching up to touch a switch along the top of the glasses from time to time.

"Looking for something?" Jacob asked.

"Gruskers," the man replied. Jacob remembered learning in school about the large herd animals that wandered the plains. "Seen any?" the man asked.

"I don't know what they look like," Jacob said. "I don't think so."

"You'd know them if you saw them," the man said, stripping off his goggles, his back still to Jacob.

"What do you want with them?" Jacob asked.

"I'm hunting them."

"What for?"

"What do you care?" the man asked, suddenly turning with a frown.

"Just curious," Jacob said, his voice shrinking almost to a whisper.

14

"For food. I like to catch my own food," the man replied, his tone softening. "A single grusker goes a long way."

"What's that?" Jacob asked, pointing to the stick now cradled in the man's arm.

"It's a rifle," he said, then added, as if anticipating Jacob's next question, "It's for the gruskers. And for anyone who decides to give me trouble." His eyes narrowed at these last words as Jacob's widened, though Jacob noticed a slight smile seemed to form along the man's mouth.

"So, what about you?" the man asked. "What are you looking for, Blinder?"

Jacob was startled at the label. "I'm not a Blinder," he said. "I'm a Seer, like you."

The man snorted. "You may be able to see, but you're not one of us. I know where you're from. It's plain enough."

Jacob wondered how much to tell him. He needed his help, but how did he know he could trust the man?

"I'm looking for the city," he said. "The big one. Where the Seers live."

The man nodded. "Well, you're headed in the right direction, then." He walked past Jacob again, heading for his craft.

Jacob followed behind, almost running to match the man's long stride.

"Wait!" he shouted.

The man halted and turned so abruptly Jacob nearly collided with him. He looked down at Jacob expectantly.

"I . . . I was hoping," Jacob stammered, "that you might be able to take me there."

The man gave a long sigh and nodded, as if he had been waiting for this all along.

"I can't. I've got things I have to do," he said, and

15

turned back toward the craft.

"Oh . . ." Jacob said. He didn't know what else to say.

"Don't give me that," the man replied, as if Jacob had broken into a desperate plea. "I've taken on more than my share of charity cases lately," he added.

The man reached up into the cab and pulled out a container. He tossed it over to Jacob, who caught it, almost falling over in surprise at its weight. Hearing a sloshing sound inside, Jacob unscrewed the cap with shaking fingers and immediately lifted it to his mouth, not even pausing to examine the contents. It was liquid, it was wet. It was water. Somewhat warm, a bit stale, with a slight taste of plastic, but Jacob decided it was the best water he'd ever had, as he guzzled it down.

"Slow down," the man barked. "You'll make yourself sick."

Jacob lowered the jug—already there was a clenching pain in his stomach. The stranger was right. Jacob offered the jug back.

"Keep it," the man said. He reached into one of the pouches along his belt and pulled out a small package, tossing it to Jacob. Wrapped in a shiny material, the parcel was no more than five inches long.

"Something to eat," the man explained. Jacob looked up questioningly. "Doesn't look like much," he acknowledged. "Powerful stuff, though. Enough for a whole day."

He pulled a few more out and tossed them over. "Tastes like the bark of a zephyr, but they'll hold you."

The man climbed up into the cockpit and buckled himself in. Putting his goggles back on, he looked down at Jacob.

"Listen, Blinder, don't worry. You'll be fine. Just keep

16

going in the direction you're headed. You'll get there soon enough."

"How far is it?" Jacob asked.

"Close. Closer than you think," he replied.

The door lowered with a hiss and the engine growled to life, throbbing so loudly Jacob had to cover his ears. The man gave Jacob a little wave, but before he could wave back, the craft was off, hurtling south once more. The grass swayed wildly in its wake. A moment later, it was gone.

Jacob reached down to pick up one of the foil packages lying in the grass.

So that's what Seers are like, he thought.

He had never felt so alone.

CHAPTER THREE

A day later, Jacob knew he'd been duped. At every rise, he kept expecting to see a city, but each time he was greeted with nothing but another set of swells stretching to the next distant ridge. He wasn't exactly sure what he was looking for, but at this point anything different from the plain would be a relief. What would a city of Seers look like, anyway? The people of Harmony lived underground in homes dug into the hillsides. With no need for windows, the design was simple and efficient, requiring few materials. The few standing structures in the community, mostly public buildings, were made of either steel or concrete, solid blocks, dull and colorless. He imagined the Seers' homes were above the surface, translucent and full of light, open to the world and to each other. Still, when it came to the Seers, he wasn't sure. This strange man had told him that the city was close, yet here he was, an afternoon later and nothing had changed.

If the man had lied, at least he'd given Jacob the means to go on. The stranger had been right about the food. The compact bar of dry and oddly chewy material didn't taste very good—in fact, it was like chewing on the frayed edges of his tunic—but it filled the hollow place inside his stomach. Eating just half a bar had carried him all the way through until this morning. He had finished the rest of it on waking, and only now was he starting to feel hungry again. Still, why hadn't the man been willing to give him a ride? What was so important that he couldn't help a person in need?

Jacob's disappointment made him even more determined to go on, and in this sense he was grateful to the man. With a twinge of shame he thought back to yesterday when, driven by hunger and thirst, by the weakness of his body, he'd been ready to give up, had even started to turn back for Harmony. Now more than ever he wanted to find other Seers, to make his way to the city and confirm what he felt to be true: *They can't all be like that man*, he told himself, pausing midstride. *I'll find the good ones. And Delaney will be with them.*

He set off again with new vigor, a steady march for the next rise. It was about half a mile away and loomed larger than the high ridge he had sweated up not long after his encounter with the Seer the day before.

He was halfway across a great basin set between two ridges. Places like this often held the promise of water. Having finished the last of what was in the stranger's jug a few hours ago, he kept an ear out for the sound of a trickle as he walked, casting his gaze back and forth in hopes of spotting a stray puddle of water.

A brightness in the grass to the right caught his eye. He froze, trying to figure out what it could be. It wasn't moving. Maybe it was a flower of some kind, he thought, though all the flowers he'd seen so far were the normal blossoms that seemed to cover the entire planet. It looked too big to be a flower.

Walking over to it, a prickling sensation passed through Jacob, traveling up his spine to the back of his neck where the hairs stood on end. He didn't know why, but he suddenly didn't want to get any closer to the object in the grass. From here he could see more white, mixed with something darker. Breathing quickly, he pushed aside the grass and gazed down at the pale fragments spread across the ground before him.

They were bones. Jacob had never seen bones before, but he had learned about them in school and these had to be them. For a moment he just stared, fascinated. He would never have imagined these solid pieces of legs and arms wrapped in flesh could gleam so brightly in the sun. Examining the length of the figure, he suddenly shivered. The shape they made was easy enough to recognize. The person had died lying facedown. The back of the skull was a pale globe. The arms were stretched forward and bent before the head, seeming to clutch the earth. The rotten remains of shoes obscured the feet. But what truly made him shiver were the tattered remnants of clothes still clinging to the body. They were faded by the sun, falling apart in places to expose the ribs and pelvis, but he could still recognize the familiar shape of the smock, the remains of a tunic like his own.

He had to be sure. With shaking hands he reached down and turned the body over, and then jumped back. The bones of the top half of the figure crumbled, falling softly to the grass, while the bottom half remained secure. The smock ripped as well, but there—along what was once the chest, still clinging to the rotting fabric—shone the gleaming disk of a sounder.

He turned away and closed his eyes. He could still see the skull staring up into the sky, its eye sockets deep, not quite circular, not quite square, its open jaw full of yellow teeth.

He can't hurt you, he told himself.

His eyes snapped open. How did he know it was a he? Could it have been a she? Could it be . . . ?

He tore his backpack off and opened the top with trembling fingers. He tipped it upside down and emptied the contents, grasping at the finder as it fell into the grass. Holding it before him, he croaked out the name.

"Delaney Corrow."

Facing the body, he felt a moment of queasiness as the pulsing started. He rotated left, away from the body in the direction he'd been traveling. A wave of relief came over him as the signal intensified. He tried again just to make sure, turning in a complete circle. It wasn't her. He didn't know what had happened to her, but this wasn't her.

Considering it further, he realized it couldn't be her. He didn't know how long it would take for a body to dissolve to bone, but he imagined it would take more than the few weeks since Delaney had left Harmony.

He went over to his pack. As he gathered up the scattered contents of the bag, he tried not to imagine Delaney stumbling through the grass blind and alone. He tried to think of something else about her instead, something happy, something he could hold onto. But it was hard. She had been so sad, so desperate the past few months. He remembered the argument he'd overheard her having with her father not long before she'd disappeared. She'd said she wanted to know what the outside world was like, had even voiced a desperate desire to see. Jacob could still hear the slap as her father reacted in rage. The next day was the last time he'd heard her voice, felt the softness of her hands. Her father had told them all that she was dead, but on his last night in Harmony, Jacob had learned the truth.

21

Closing up his pack, he glanced over at the remains once more. He couldn't help but wonder—if it wasn't Delaney, then who was it? Obviously, he or she had, like both him and Delaney, fled Harmony. Was it someone he had known growing up? Maybe it had been someone like him, someone who had regained his or her sight. Thinking of the difficulties his own journey had yielded, it seemed impossible that someone blind could make it so far, would even know which direction to go. Then again, in the end the person hadn't made it, had ended up here for Jacob to stumble across months or even years later.

Sitting down to rest, he stared over at the body, no longer afraid, just sad. What had this person's final moments been like? What kind of suffering had they felt? What kind of suffering had driven them to strike out blindly, to risk an ending like this? How could anyone blind think they could make it?

He had to believe they could. He had to believe Delaney could.

Jacob went back to the body and reached down, gingerly retrieving the anonymous sounder. It tore away easily from the rags. Tilting it back and forth against the sun so that it flashed a pattern against his tunic, he smiled briefly. This daring person would not be lost forever. He or she would, in some little way, be remembered.

As he placed the sounder in his pack, a thought struck him: His whole life, he had never even considered that anyone would actually leave Harmony, let alone want to. Yet now he knew of at least two people—three, including himself—who had done so. How many more were there? He thought back to his last night in Harmony. Under the light of the ringed moon he had wandered out to the burial grounds to say good-bye to Delaney. He remembered the vast expanse of pathminders laid out in a grid to mark the resting places of the dead. Delaney's grave was empty. How many others were as well?

As he hoisted his pack and turned to resume his journey, an odd sensation made him raise his eyes. It felt like the pulsing of his sounder, though the throbbing was fainter and was coming up from the ground through his feet. He looked around but saw nothing. For a moment he thought of yesterday's hum that heralded the arrival of the strange craft. Maybe the man had changed his mind and was coming back for him.

There was a distant bellow in the south. He turned and saw a host of dark shapes sliding over the hill into the basin, heading in his direction. For a minute Jacob watched, puzzled. They didn't move nearly as fast as the man's vehicle had, but they were moving fast enough. And there were a lot of them—by now too many for Jacob to count as still more poured over the horizon.

Gruskers.

The stranger had said Jacob would know them when he saw them, and he was right. They were still a ways off but closing quickly, and though he didn't seem to remember learning they were dangerous, he didn't know how they might react to him. All he knew was that they were much bigger than he was.

The shaking underfoot intensified. He began jogging, then racing, up the steady incline toward the high ridge ahead as the sound of the gruskers—one long roll of thundering hooves accented by the bellowing of many voices—filled the valley. Running out of breath, he chanced a look over his shoulder. The creatures were a good fifty yards away and no longer moving in his direction. What's more, the herd had slowed, spreading out to graze as the last of them entered the basin. Stopping to catch his breath, he turned and dropped back into the grass. He gazed down across the basin, captivated by the scene.

The huge herbivores paid him no mind as he watched. He had never seen animals so big. Dark in hue with brilliant stripes and four massive tusks that emerged from the sides of their head to cover their face like a cage, they dwarfed the sheep and cattle Jacob had seen at Harmony. He had learned about the gruskers last year in school when they studied native species, and he had heard their cries on the rare occasion they passed near the perimeter of the colony, but they were far more beautiful and impressive by sight than he could have imagined in his blindness. For an hour he observed them as they headed north, intersecting his own path. Pausing individually here and there to browse, the whole herd moved with a distinct rhythm, and because their legs were almost totally obscured by the high vegetation, they appeared to float through the landscape, leaving a wake of trodden and cropped grass. Somewhere amid the mass of creatures lay the lost Blinder. Jacob hoped the bones would remain undisturbed.

Watching the gruskers, he was reminded of the starship he'd seen his last night in Harmony, floating against the star field, drifting into space. As with the ship, he wondered where the gruskers were going. Did they, too, have a destination, or were they wandering without aim? He imagined the latter. They didn't need a destination—wherever they were, that was where they were supposed to be. They were lucky.

Yes, he had a destination, a reason to move on, but with it came the burden of finding it. They, on the other hand, had no sense of urgency, no fear.

Most of all, the gruskers had their herd. They had each other. They didn't travel alone.

And what was he? He was nothing. Just a boy drifting on a sea of grass, a single speck barely visible against the indifferent plain.

He rose and continued on his way, leaving the gruskers to their grazing. But as the slope steepened, forcing him to lean in against the incline, reaching forward for tufts of grass to help pull him up the face of the ridge, his thoughts drifted back to the creatures, his envy sharpening at the sounds of their calling to one another. The calls pushed his mind back farther, all the way across five days of journeying through the plain, back to Harmony.

He tried to imagine what was happening there right now. Ever since he'd left, he'd been wondering what his people had been told about his disappearance. Did they know what he'd done? How would the knowledge affect them? Maybe they didn't know. Maybe he had received the same treatment as Delaney—another lost child to be buried and then forgotten. Most of all, he wondered about his parents. He tried to imagine his mother at this moment, sitting at the table in the darkness of the house, alone. Losing Delaney, who had been as much a daughter to her as an apprentice, had been devastating enough. Could she tolerate yet another loss? Was his father there for her right now? Did she even want him there? Jacob still remembered the sight of her secretly embracing the high councilor, and he remembered the constant fighting of his parents, the tension between them over the last year.

But he also remembered them walking together before him on the way back from the council chamber, where he'd been revealed as a Seer—they had joined hands in a moment of intimacy that seemed to carry over to the next day. How strange would it be if the event that had torn Jacob from his parents was what brought them together? All he knew was that he missed both of them now more than ever. . . .

A sudden roar shook Jacob. He looked up to see a triangular ship passing over him, its engines flaring. A second later, it disappeared over the ridge. He took a few deep breaths to try to steady his shaking body and remember where he was. Blood pounded in his ears.

To his surprise he found himself almost at the top of the hill. Over the course of his daydream he had nearly finished the ascent.

He broke into a run, hoping to catch another sight of the ship. As he rounded the ridge's summit, his eyes caught sight of the other side, its steep incline stretching below him. He froze.

At the base of the long slope the scenery shifted. Groves of dark trees—some large enough to be called forests—dotted the landscape, breaking up the uniformity of the plains. Below him lay a body of water much larger than the few tiny ponds he had encountered. The lake stretched long and thin on the floor of the depression, and he could see variations of depth in the different hues across its length. The center was dark and deep, while along its edges the shallows reflected the lighter shades of sky. From this distance he could distinguish the oval shapes of two glinting craft at the northern shore, where a grove of dark trees spread out to encircle the whole end of the lake. His breath quickened at the shapes of moving figures against the sand.

The sight of people so close, however, was soon over-whelmed as his gaze continued to the horizon. There the constant edge where plain met sky was broken by another glint, this time of towers and buildings. He watched the great ship shrink as it cruised toward the city.

He had finally arrived.

CHAPTER FOUR

Creeping through the shadows, Jacob headed toward the sunlight, toward the voices just beyond the trees. Their words, while indistinct, were light and loud, punctuated with laughter. At the edge of the grove he settled behind a trunk and studied the people only a few dozen yards away. He kept his head down, remembering he was no longer invisible, the way he'd been in Harmony.

There were eight of them—four men and four women—though when he looked more closely, he noticed they appeared to be only about four or five years older than him, maybe Delaney's age. Two of the girls and a boy huddled talking on a blanket by one of the gleaming craft at the edge of the water. The other five were closer to him.

They were the opposite of the Seer he'd met yesterday, in both appearance and attitude. That man had been dark in complexion, fully dressed for the hunt. And whereas he had been somber and serious, they were anything but. They romped in the sand, laughing and shouting as they played some kind of game, batting a glowing sphere back and forth. The ball floated of its own accord; when they hit it in midair, it streaked around them, leaving a tracer of light that lasted a second before fading.

As for their appearance—Jacob blinked as he stared from one to another. They all looked the same. Both the boys and the girls had light, slicked-back hair that seemed to blend in with their tanned bodies. Their faces were round with small, symmetrical features. They wore scanty clothes, a few strips of fabric the same tone as their hair and skin, giving them the appearance of animated statues.

As he watched them play, their tall, muscular bodies kicking around the sand, Jacob suddenly felt awkward and self-conscious. *Is this what all the other Seers look like?* he wondered. He stared at his own tunic, fraying at the edges, stained by grass and sweat, and remembered his reflection in the pool, his rough features and uncombed hair. For a moment he debated whether to bypass this group and keep going, to push on to the city in the distance, but he realized that was foolish—he would have to get help from someone at some point. They seemed friendly, more so than yesterday's Seer. Besides, he could spot near the trio lying on the shore what looked like a picnic of sorts on their blanket.

He stepped from the grove, softly, quietly, and approached the group.

They failed to notice him at first. Then the players, one by one, stopped their game and turned, staring. Even the sphere, its brilliant tracer melting into air, seemed to be watching him as it hovered in place. No one said a word. The awkwardness of the moment seemed tangible, itself a sphere that hovered in the air, encompassing all of them.

"Hello," Jacob said, and tried waving like the man had done yesterday, not sure what else to do.

No one answered. He felt their eyes moving over him,

absorbing every quality. By now the group sitting off to the side had joined the others.

"Is he security?" a girl asked a boy next to her.

"Can't be. He's younger than us. And I mean—look at him," the boy responded.

"Who is he then, Garrett?" another boy asked him.

"How should I know?" Garrett retorted.

"You idiots," another girl interjected. "Why don't you ask him? Hey, you, what are you doing here?"

Jacob wasn't sure how to address the golden group. "I've been walking," he finally said, trying not to stammer. "I saw your ships." He felt foolish and awkward.

"You came all the way from Melville?" a girl asked, her voice brimming with vacuous awe. "That's a long way to come for a swim."

"Don't be silly, Raelyn," said the girl who had chastised them earlier. "He would have had to leave last night to get all the way out here, and I don't see any other skimmer around, do you? Besides, look at his clothes. Even the base workers don't dress like that."

They murmured in agreement. The girl turned her gaze to Jacob.

"So, where *are* you coming from?" she asked him, smiling.

"From Harmony," he answered. "I've been walking for a few days."

At this they began whispering to one another excitedly, glancing at him sideways, except for a boy who continued staring with a puzzled look. "Harmony? Is that a place or something?"

"Taylor," the girl informed him, "Harmony's the other

30

colony. You know—where the Blinders live?"

"Oh, yeah!" Taylor said, brightening.

"No way, Coral," Garrett said. "He can obviously see, so therefore he isn't a Blinder." He smiled at Coral, proud of his logic.

They all turned back to Jacob, silently waiting for an explanation.

"I can see," Jacob said. He didn't want to lie, but he felt hesitant, not certain how much to tell them. "Somehow I began to see. I'm not sure why. That's why I had to leave."

To his surprise, they seemed perfectly satisfied with the explanation. A few of them returned to their game, and soon they were running around in the sand once more, laughing as before, as if he hadn't appeared at all.

"Are you hungry?" Coral asked him. "Come over to the blanket and have some lunch." She motioned to Jacob to follow her to the food, and he went eagerly. Another girl tagged along. They sat together on the blanket while the others played. Jacob dove into the food, stuffing his mouth with fruit and some sort of pastry filled with cheese and a kind of spicy meat. He didn't know if it was the food's quality or the fact that he had eaten nothing the last three days except those dry bars, but it all tasted better than anything he had ever eaten before. The two girls watched in amazement as he gobbled everything down. He was so hungry he barely noticed their smiles as they struggled not to giggle. When he was finished, they asked him his name.

"Well, Jacob," Coral said, "my name's Coral and she's Raelyn. Over there are Garrett, Taylor, Marcus, Pell, Celine, and Irena." She quickly pointed at each one as she rattled off the names; Jacob had difficulty following her.

31

"So, you really were a Blinder?" Raelyn asked. "Interesting."

"I know," Coral said. "Wait till we get back to Melville and tell the others. They're going to be so jealous."

"Why?" Jacob asked. He was a little surprised. He tried to imagine how his own people would've reacted if a Seer had suddenly shown up in their midst. With a pang he realized that he had already found out.

"Because, silly," Raelyn laughed, "Blinders are so strange, and no one's allowed to go see them."

"I've asked Daddy so many times to let me go, but he says it's against the law. Some treaty or something. Anyway, meeting a Blinder is just, well, something different," Coral added.

"Yeah," Raelyn said. "If you haven't noticed, this planet's so boring."

"Oh," Jacob replied.

Soon the two girls were engaged in conversation and seemed to forget him. Between the food and the walking, he was suddenly sleepy. Letting them talk, he lay back on the warm sand. For the first time in a long time he felt his body relax. Everything was going to be okay. These strangers would help him, would take him to the city. It was a good place to start. He closed his eyes and rested, only half listening to their conversation.

Filtered through his drowsiness, the timbre of the girls' voices reminded him of Delaney. She came upon him in the darkness, a memory of her sounding in his ear. Suddenly he was back in Harmony before anything had changed, when he was still blind, and she was still happy.

They were at the piano. His mother had gone out on an errand after Delaney's lesson and the two of them had spent an hour playing guesser, taking turns molding little figures out of clay while the other deduced the shape. Jacob had been busy forming a cat, listening to Delaney tell one of her favorite stories, when she suddenly stopped and pulled him over to the piano.

"What are you doing?" he asked, the clay still in his hands.

"I almost forgot," she said. "I have something to play for you."

She began. It was a slow song, rhythmic and sweet, a waltz so pure it could have been a child's lullaby. They were both quiet for a long time after she finished.

"That was amazing," he said at last.

"You like it? I wrote it for you, Jacob."

"For me?"

"That's right. The other night I was sitting at home and I thought of you. And that's when I sat down and wrote it. It's a very special song." She put her arm around him.

"It is," he agreed.

Jacob smiled now at the memory. It wasn't long after that that Delaney's mood began to change, when she started getting sad all the time and darker in her criticisms of her father and the others. Jacob wished he had listened more.

A strange prickle suddenly burned across his forehead. His body, which just a moment ago had felt so relaxed, tensed as all the muscles in his back stiffened. For a moment he thought it was the memory of Delaney that had disturbed him, but taking a deep breath he realized it was something else, something beyond him, a darkness gnawing at the edges of the quiet.

He tuned back in to the girls' conversation and tried to

forget the sensation that had already begun to subside. For nearly half an hour they babbled nonstop. They discussed school and their parents, all of whom seemed to work together for someone or something called Mixel. They talked about parties they had recently attended, people they liked and disliked. They watched their friends, who were still running in the sun, and made funny and sarcastic observations about them. They even talked a little about him, apparently thinking he was asleep. They seemed to feel sorry for him because of his clothes and because he had been a Blinder. It felt awkward listening to their conversation. There was a strict rule against eavesdropping in Harmony. He didn't think the same rules applied here, but he couldn't shake the feeling he was doing something wrong. Maybe that was the source of the lingering uneasiness.

He was about to stir and pretend to wake when he heard Raelyn say, "I just remembered. He's like that girl. Remember, the one we heard the other night at the party?"

"That's right. I almost forgot. I wonder if he knows her?" Coral asked.

Before he could ask them what they meant, a whine sounded in the distance, and the girls stopped their conversation as the noise grew. He sat up, blinking. Shading his eyes with his hand, he looked around for the source, feeling his body stiffen once again. The prickling had returned.

"What's that sound?" Jacob asked.

"A floater, I think," Coral replied. "Someone's coming."

"Who could have followed us out here?" Raelyn asked.

The girls stood up and walked over to where the others now congregated at the water's edge. Their sudden solemnity made Jacob even more nervous. The hum intensified and a craft emerged over the far ridge from the direction of the city. It was similar in shape to the ones parked on the beach but smaller, its surface decorated with alternating stripes that angled into slim Vs along its sides. It floated over the terrain, leaving the grass swirling behind it, and skimmed over the water.

Jacob rose and joined the others, sidling up to Coral. Suddenly, he didn't want to be back there on the blanket alone.

"Oh, great," said Marcus. "Looks like Turner and those other two."

"Garrett, did you invite those creeps out here?" Celine demanded, slapping him.

"Ow!" Garrett said, rubbing his shoulder. "Of course not. You think I want those losers around?"

"Who's Turner?" Jacob asked, stepping in closer to Coral.

Coral looked down at him. "Turner's some older guy Garrett met a few months ago back when he had a taste for the black market. Works at the port. Knows all the smugglers. Now he and his friends won't leave us alone."

"They think they're tough," Pell snorted.

"They *are* tough, Pell," Irena said. "You saw what they did to that kid Zach, didn't you? I even heard they killed someone."

"That's not true," Garrett broke in, laughing. "Turner started that rumor himself. As for Zach, he had it coming, you all know that. Look, they're only a year older than us, maybe two. Forget how they seem. They're harmless. Besides, they know that if they gave any of us trouble, my father would have them all fired and deported before they could say Mixel."

The group seemed to relax at Garrett's words—everyone except Jacob.

Skirting the surface, the craft sped to the center of the lake and pulled a hard turn, circling into a tighter and tighter spin that caused a spray of water to erupt like a fountain. Coral, Garrett, and the others on the beach began cheering sarcastically and laughing, raising their hands in mock salute. The skimmer then came to a stop, turned, and moved toward them in a slow, deliberate manner.

"Garrett, I thought you told these guys to stop coming around," Taylor said.

"Well, I meant to," Garrett replied. "There was just never a good time."

The group gave a collective groan.

"Relax, people," Garrett said confidently, "I know they're trudges, but like I told you before, they're harmless. Just humor them and they'll go away."

The craft had closed most of the distance by now. From where he stood, Jacob could distinguish three young men in the floater. The driver and the kid sitting in the backseat both sported long dark hair that flapped behind them in the breeze. The one next to the driver had short, spiky hair, light in color. They looked pale in comparison to the group waiting on the beach, and all three wore dark glasses that obscured their eyes. Watching them draw near, Jacob was suddenly reminded of the skull he'd seen back on the other side of the ridge.

"Ugh," Celine groaned. "They're so creepy."

"Just smile, dammit," Garrett said, breaking into a grin himself as he waved to the approaching trio.

The craft pulled onto the sand and stopped opposite from where the group stood. The boys inside took their time getting out, laughing and talking quietly to one another as if they were having some vital conversation that had to be concluded.

Jacob winced, realizing he was clenching his fists so tightly that his fingernails were biting into his palms. *I should have kept going,* he thought to himself. *Being here is a mistake.* No—the others didn't seem worried. He had to trust his new friends. They wouldn't let anything happen.

Wearing jumpsuits that resembled some kind of uniform, the three climbed from the floater and jumped onto the sand, landing like cats. They sauntered over with leering grins.

"Garre. Good to see you," the man with short, spiked hair said. His voice was surprisingly gentle and smooth. His words seemed to hang in the air before melting away like smoke.

"What's up, Turner," Garrett responded with a nod.

"Nice suits, ladies," Turner said, bowing in their direction. The girls turned to each other and smirked. Coral rolled her eyes. Irena let out a snorting giggle. Turner took no notice and continued. "Nice place you picked out, kids. Peaceful. Private. Away from the city."

"We like it," Garrett said. "Just found this place a month ago."

"Who's that?" Turner suddenly demanded, pointing at Jacob. Jacob could feel himself shrinking and wished he could disappear. His pulse thudded in his ears.

"Nobody. Just some kid who showed up," Garrett said. "Hey, Turner, how'd you find us?"

"Cuts right to the chase. I like that," Turner said. He put his arm around Garrett, who seemed to shrink under its weight. "Who says we were looking for you? Got off our shift not too long ago. Decided we'd go for a nice skim out in the country. Fresh air and all that, right?"

37

"Right," Garrett said, sidling from under Turner's arm.

Turner laughed. "You don't mind if we join you, do you Garre? Looks like you're having fun. A real good time here."

Jacob shifted from foot to foot, listening to Turner's voice. It was so slow, laid back almost, yet with an acidic quality that dissolved whatever he said, cutting the words down to a razor tip. Jacob couldn't tell if Turner was picking up on Garrett's reticence or not. It seemed that he must. But why would he choose to ignore it? Jacob didn't understand, but it made him uneasy.

"Well, Turner," Garrett said, struggling to assume confidence, "you can do what you want, but I think we're probably leaving soon, so there's really no point in sticking around. Right, guys?" he asked, turning to the others for support.

Coral stepped forward. "I think what Garrett's trying to tell you creeps is that he wants you to leave and not bother us anymore, right *Garre*?"

"Coral!" Garrett snapped.

Jacob gasped. So did a few of the others. Turner's two friends looked over at each other, trying to decide how to react.

Turner let out a long, slow laugh and grinned, even as his face darkened to a deep shade of red.

For a moment, everyone was still, casting nervous glances all around. Coral had broken the spell and it couldn't be remade. Even Jacob felt it. Garrett appeared to be the only one who failed to understand.

"Don't listen to her, Turner. She's just running her mouth."

"Shut up," Turner snapped, his face souring. "You think I don't know? Sure, as long as I could get you the things you wanted you were happy enough to come around. Too bad you had to go slumming like that, huh?"

He advanced upon Garrett, who shrank at his approach, and pulled back his fist as if to throw a punch. Garrett winced, which drew laughter from Turner and his two friends. Jacob breathed a sigh of relief as Turner spun and walked away from Garrett. He motioned to the other two, and they headed toward their floater. But he hadn't gone far when Coral called out again.

"Next time you're lugging boxes at the port, look inside one—maybe you'll find a brain!"

Turner looked back over his shoulder as he strode away, a string of expletives spewing from his mouth, too distracted to notice the rock jutting out of the sand in front of him. His foot caught, sending him face-first into the ground. Garrett, Coral, and the others burst out laughing, not stopping even as Turner picked himself up, spitting out sand.

Stop laughing, Jacob pleaded in his mind. *Leave him alone and he'll go away.*

But it was too late. Furious, Turner whirled and once more advanced upon the group, pulling something from the pocket of his jumpsuit. The laughter died. They all stepped back with a gasp.

"He's got a gun!" Celine cried, pointing to the object in Turner's hand.

Turner menaced the pistol before them. "You like laughing? Let's hear you laugh. Come on!"

The group was silent.

"No? So what are you going to do—go crying to Mommy and Daddy? Don't even think about it. I know enough dirt to get you all in plenty of trouble, courtesy of Garrett. You think you're so glamorous? You make me sick," he sneered. He surveyed the group, all of whom looked down, their faces now blank.

Jacob stood to the side, watching in shock as the spectacle unfolded. Suddenly, Turner's eyes locked with his own, narrowing to slits.

"What I don't get," Turner said, striding toward Jacob as he pocketed his pistol, "is why we're not good enough to be in your sight for two minutes, yet you let this dirty little piece of garbage hang around."

Jacob tried to back away, but Turner was too quick. His hand reached out and struck Jacob squarely on the chest, sending him sprawling backward onto the sand.

"Come on, get up," Turner snarled. When Jacob hesitated, Turner grabbed him by the front of his shirt and dragged him to his feet. Jacob looked into his eyes but couldn't tell what he saw. Was it hate? Fear? Bitterness? He wasn't sure. He wasn't even scared anymore. The whole scene was too surreal, leaving him with a strange feeling of detachment, as if none of this were really happening to him.

Turner slapped him hard across the face, knocking him to the ground once more. Pain drew Jacob back. Suddenly, the moment was all too real. Reaching up to his throbbing nose, he felt a wetness. He pulled his hand away, staring at the blood's brilliance. How did he become the target? He turned to Coral and the others for help.

They looked away in silence. A few even headed back to the blanket to begin packing up. Turner snorted.

"How do you like your new friends now?" he said, pulling Jacob back to his feet.

"Let him go," a voice called out behind Jacob. He had

heard that voice before. Turner looked up and a flicker of surprise crossed his face. Jacob peered over his shoulder and saw the man he'd met yesterday advance from the edge of the clearing.

"Who the hell are you?" Turner demanded.

"Nobody. Just like him," the man replied, pointing to Jacob as he closed in.

"He's with you?"

"That's right," the man said. He now stood before them. "So let him go."

"I don't believe this," Turner said. He shook his head and glanced around. Everyone was quiet, watching. Suddenly, he looked back, sneering. "No. I don't feel like it."

The man's arm shot out, broke Turner's grip, grabbed Jacob, and hauled him around behind him, all in one fluid motion.

Swearing, Turner yanked his pistol out and raised it. Jacob's eyes widened at the sight of it hanging, shaking, only inches from the man's face.

Jacob thought he saw a flicker of a smile, perhaps the slightest flare of the nostrils. Other than that, the man never flinched. Then there was a blur of movement. One moment Turner and the stranger stood on opposite sides of the pistol, the next Turner was writhing on the ground, unable to speak, his pistol now in the stranger's hand. As Turner twisted at his feet, the man looked down and adjusted a dial on the gun.

Turner's friends cried out and scrambled to produce their own weapons. Jacob was going to call out a warning, but before he could, the stranger pointed Turner's pistol at one and calmly pulled the trigger. A white flash erupted, striking the young man full on. Before he even hit the ground, the stranger brought the gun to bear on the other. There was another flash, and he collapsed as well. Jacob stared in horror as both of them convulsed in rhythm to the web of energy entangling them. A moment later the web faded, leaving Turner's friends still. Turner had stopped contorting and now lay facedown, groaning.

There was a humming of engines. Jacob looked over to the shore. At the first shot, the bronzed youths had scattered for their floaters with a chorus of screams. Jacob watched them finish piling in before taking off across the water. A moment later, Garrett, Coral, Taylor, Raelyn, and the rest were gone.

Looking around, the man shook his head in disgust. "Bunch of fools," he said. "All of them."

Jacob crumpled into the sand. He wanted to throw up. When he closed his eyes he could still see the two youths convulsing. The blood from his nose had seeped into his mouth. He could taste its metal saltiness on his tongue. He opened his eyes again and watched the stranger.

The man walked over to one of the motionless figures and prodded him gently with his foot. He bent down and put his fingers against the young man's throat.

"Are they dead?" Jacob managed to croak.

Rising, the man shook his head. "Though I wouldn't want to be them in a few hours," he added. He reached into the youth's pocket and pulled out the pistol, then walked over and picked up the one that had fallen at the other boy's feet. He pitched them both, along with Turner's, into the lake, where they landed one after another with a loud plunk.

"Amateurs," he muttered. He turned and marched past Jacob toward the woods.

42

Jacob didn't notice him as he went by. He just stared down, watching the sand absorb his drops of blood. There was a long silence.

"Hey, Blinder," the man called out.

Jacob raised his head. The stranger stood at the edge of the clearing.

"Are you coming or not?"

CHAPTER FIVE

Jacob clung to the bars surrounding him, gritting his teeth as the vibrations of the cruiser bounced him around the backseat. The throttle roared in his ears. He looked out, watching the land slip by.

After following the stranger through the trees, weaving up the valley for nearly half a mile, they had arrived at a small clearing where the dark green craft from yesterday waited, looking beat-up in comparison with the teens' sleek floaters. Without a word, the stranger had hoisted Jacob into the seat behind the cockpit, jumped in the front, and taken off, plowing through the high grass, then turning onto a road of sorts where the ground had been worn flat.

At the path he veered left and accelerated. Jacob had never ridden in any kind of transport, let alone one that moved so quickly, and his stomach rose and fell with every hill. They didn't travel long, maybe ten minutes. At first, Jacob thought they were going to the city—at each rise he could see it before them. But toward the end of the trip the stranger turned off the trail and onto another that seemed equally used.

Already sick to his stomach, Jacob again began to panic. He'd had no control over anything that had happened to him today. Numb with shock by the fight at the lake, he had followed the stranger's instructions like an automaton. But now, with nothing to do except cling for dear life in the backseat, he had plenty of time to think about what was happening. He still had no idea who this man was or where he was taking him. All he knew was that the man was dangerous—more dangerous than Turner and his friends put together. Yet, he had saved him, hadn't he?

Before he had any more time to wonder, the cruiser turned between two hills. Beyond, the area opened into a meadow dotted with the same kind of trees Jacob had seen at the lake. They passed into the shade of a large copse and emerged on the other side, where a house squatted on the side of a rise. A deck encircled the front. The dwelling was different from the buildings in Harmony; the face was comprised of large panes of glass, and the structure wasn't made of metal, but a smooth material that gave the house an earthier look than the industrial buildings of Harmony. The cruiser pulled up before the house. The man exited the driver's seat and approached Jacob.

"You look a little green," the man remarked, looking him over. "I guess the ride's a bit rough when you're not used to it." As always, his face was blank, offering neither sympathy nor hostility. Jacob didn't move. The man spoke again. "Well, you can stay in there if you want, but you'd probably be more comfortable down here."

Jacob stood up, and the man helped him down onto the ground. He steadied himself against the side of the cruiser. He noticed that his hands were shaking; in fact, his whole body trembled.

"All in one piece, don't worry," the man said.

"I don't understand," Jacob said. The ground beneath him was beginning to settle, but his mind was still a whirl of confusion, anger, and fear. "Why did you save me back there?"

"You're welcome."

"Well, yesterday you didn't. You just left me to keep going."

"Guess I should have done the same today," the man snapped.

"Well, if you had picked me up yesterday, none of that would have happened. That's all I'm saying," Jacob mumbled. He figured it was foolish to challenge the stranger, but he was too tired and sore to care.

"You didn't need my help yesterday. And you wouldn't have today if that idiot Turner and his two cronies hadn't shown up. Anyway, like I told you, I had things to do." The man scowled. "Besides, why should I be responsible for every person I come across who's stupid enough to wander the plains alone?"

Jacob looked down and didn't respond. Instead, he blinked back tears, trying not to give in. The afternoon was catching up with him—the violence, the shallowness and cruelty of the teens, the indifference of this man—all of it crashing down in a wave that threatened to wash him away. *They were right,* was all he could think. *My teachers, my parents, everyone. Everything they said about the Seers was true.* He was a fool.

The man sighed and went to the back of the cruiser. He retrieved a satchel and passed Jacob, heading for the house.

"I need a drink," he called back. "And we need to take care of that nose. You look like hell."

Not knowing what else to do, Jacob followed him to the

46

house. Along the way, he reached up, felt his nose, and winced. It was swollen and tender, and his face was sticky from the dried blood.

They ascended a set of steps to the deck. Jacob paused at the top. From this height the deck looked out over the meadow, where the trees rustled in the breeze, whispering to one another. In the distance he could see the city towers.

When he glanced back over his shoulder, the man was watching him.

"Like the view?" the man asked. His voice had softened.

Jacob nodded. "I'm Jacob," he said after a minute.

"I know," the man said. "I heard you tell the girls."

"You were there the whole time?" Jacob asked.

The man shrugged. "I watch people from time to time," he said. "You probably know what that's like," he added. "Right?"

Jacob looked down. He felt himself blush but said nothing.

"I'm Xander," the man said at last. "Alexander, really. But I go by Xander." He turned and walked inside. Jacob followed.

The house was spare and neatly arranged. Most of the interior was one lofty room with a kitchen, a table with benches, and two large padded chairs facing the wall of windows. A staircase along one side ascended to a balcony where several doorways led to back rooms. The opposite wall was lined with shelves housing rows of narrow, rectangular objects. While Xander went to a cabinet in the kitchen and took out two glasses and a bottle, Jacob approached the shelves and removed one of the objects. It had a cover, which he opened. Inside was gathered a stack of thin sheets made of unfamiliar material that was flexible like the thinnest cloth but much stiffer. As he flipped through them, he noticed they were filled with strangely patterned rows of markings. Xander poured a light clear liquid into each of the glasses, filling one halfway and the other less than a quarter full. He approached Jacob, carrying both glasses.

"What are these?" Jacob asked, holding up the item.

"Those are books." Xander seemed puzzled and somewhat amused by the question. "I guess Blinders wouldn't have need of them. Hell, most people probably wouldn't know what books are, anyway. They're old-fashioned. Collectibles. I've gathered most of them over the years on business. You read them—those symbols represent words."

"I've heard of reading," Jacob said. "We learned about it once in school. We don't need to read. Our recordings provide information. My teacher said it's more efficient that way."

"Right. Here, drink this," Xander said, handing Jacob the glass.

"What is it?"

"Something to help you sleep. It's medicine."

Jacob took the glass and drank it. The liquid burned in his throat and made his eyes water. "That tastes horrible," he said, choking.

"Like I said, it's medicine. Medicine always tastes bad. Now, let's get you cleaned up."

He had Jacob sit down on one of the table benches while he retrieved a small box from the bathroom just off the kitchen. Sitting down opposite from Jacob, he took a pad of soft material, soaked it in some solution from a brown bottle, and began gingerly applying it to Jacob's face. Jacob winced at the sharp pain, but soon it began to subside. He felt a mild numbness around his nose. The solution had a sharp odor that, while not unpleasant, made his nostrils prickle.

"What is that stuff?" Jacob asked.

"Cleanser," Xander said, still dabbing. Jacob could see his blood on the cloth. "It's also got a healing agent in it. The swelling should go down soon." He shook his head. "That Turner whaled you good."

"I don't understand," Jacob said. "I didn't do anything."

Xander sighed. "Doesn't matter," he said at last. "You were there. He could hit you. He couldn't hit the others."

"Why didn't they help me?"

"I don't know," Xander replied. "They're rich kids. They don't do much good or bad in the world."

He finished cleaning Jacob's face and packed everything back in the kit except for the cloth. He took it to the sink while Jacob finished what was in the glass.

"Go rest," Xander said, rinsing the cloth. "Head right up those stairs to the far room; there's a spare bed waiting for you."

"You mean I can stay?" Jacob asked.

Xander held up his hands. "Let's not get ahead of ourselves, now."

"Oh."

The man frowned. "Just go upstairs. I'll wake you for dinner."

Jacob obeyed, finding it comforting to be given orders and, most of all, to have someplace to go. By the time he reached the top of the stairs, warmth was spreading from his stomach throughout his body and lightness filled his head. He found the room and surrendered to the comfort of the bed.

• • •

A delicious aroma woke Jacob. He stretched his sore muscles before sinking back into the mattress, still drifty from sleep. Then he stiffened, seized by a moment of confusion in the darkness of the room. At last he remembered where he was, remembered everything that had happened to him since leaving Harmony—the hunger, the thirst, the fatigue, not to mention the violence and the fear—it all came rushing back. He wrapped the blanket tighter around him. It was behind him. He was safe now. He didn't really know Xander, but somehow he felt safer than he had in a long time. *Then again*, he thought, remembering the beach, *you said that before. And what happened?*

He got out of bed and went downstairs. It was dark outside; Jacob wondered how long he had slept. A few lamps cast the room in a warm glow. Going to the window, he noticed he could see his reflection in the glass. He touched his nose—it was still tender, but the swelling he'd felt earlier appeared to have gone down. When he turned around, he saw Xander watching him from the kitchen table. He seemed to have just finished eating. An empty plate lay across the table from him, with platters of food in between.

"I was about to wake you," the man said. "Food's still hot—help yourself." He rose, left the table, and stepped outside into the darkness.

Jacob sat down. He helped himself from bowls of mashed potatoes and beans and took a large piece of what tasted like beef. He wondered if it was grusker. As much as he had eaten at lunch, he felt ravenous again and stuffed himself. He couldn't remember having eaten so much food in one day. Compared with the limited portions he had been served in Harmony, this was a feast. He thought of his parents. What meager

50

dinner were they having right now? He imagined the two of them eating silently in the total darkness of the underground house.

When he finished, he brought his plate to the sink and went out onto the deck. Where had Xander gone? With the light of the house behind him, he peered into the dark. Utter blackness lay before his eyes, pressing in on him. He had spent nearly all his life in darkness, but this momentary blindness frightened him. He could see nothing before him and felt disoriented by the vastness of the night. Slowly his eyes adjusted. In the distance he could distinguish points of light on the horizon where the city lay, casting a steady glow into the sky around it.

A breeze picked up. The smell of smoke drifted into his nostrils. His heart began to pound; growing up, he had been taught to fear fire as the ultimate danger. In school they had practiced fire drills and what to do if they detected the odor of smoke. They had learned about a devastating fire in the colony thirty years ago that had destroyed much of the eastern tier before burning itself out, and about the occasional fires that swept the prairies, consuming everything in their path. Striding to the edge of the deck, Jacob looked to the right, in the direction from which the aromatic scent wafted, and spotted a flicker of light between the trees. Taking a deep breath, he told himself that it had to be Xander's fire, that it was a controlled burn.

Should he go down there? Maybe Xander wanted to be alone, but Jacob didn't. He walked down the staircase toward the light.

He passed between the trees into a small clearing. Xander sat on the far side of a circular pit lined with stones in

51

which a fire burned. The flames illuminated the clearing from below, revealing the trunks and lower limbs of the trees around them, casting shadows that danced amid the light. In the glow, Xander's face appeared to shine. His eyes sparkled beneath the recess of his brow. He motioned Jacob to sit on a stump to the left of the pit. Jacob settled down as Xander threw a few pieces of wood on the fire, releasing a cloud of sparks.

"Not much wood on this planet, but I collect the fallen pieces," the man said.

"It smells nice," Jacob replied.

"The wood of the zephyr tree."

For a few minutes neither spoke. Jacob stared at the flames flickering about the dry limbs. They crackled as they ignited, dissolving into the white light of embers. A sense of peace seemed to radiate from the focal point of light into every part of his body. The fire, constant yet ever changing, was as beautiful as anything he had seen so far.

"Have you always lived here?" Jacob asked.

"No."

"How long?"

"A while," the man said.

"Well, where did you live before?" Jacob asked. "What did you do?" So far, the man's answers weren't very helpful. "Did you use to live in that city?" The man was quiet. "On another planet?"

The man sighed at the barrage of questions. "Five years," he said at last. "I've been here five years. I used to be a soldier, a company man. Not anymore. I fought for the Mixel Corporation—they're the jerks that basically own this planet—for twenty years all around the Rim. Can't believe I'm still alive. I shouldn't be." He shook his head.

"You fought in wars?" Jacob asked.

"I wouldn't exactly call them wars. More like two kids fighting over who gets which toy. Trade routes, resources, open planets, colonization rights, franchises—everything. Most of the battles were illegal. Some of them were secret."

"So how did you get here?"

The man paused, gazing deep into the fire before answering.

"When I retired, I put in for some land here on Nova Campi, and the bastards gave it to me along with a pension. A fair exchange for all the dirty work I did for them."

"You killed people?" Jacob whispered.

"Yeah, I killed people—people who tried to kill me," Xander snapped, glancing up. He looked back into the flames. "Can't say I enjoyed it. Can't say I hated it either."

Jacob shivered, remembering how smoothly Xander had dispatched Turner and his friends. He didn't understand everything the man was telling him, but it was enough to make him uneasy. He decided to change the subject. "You must get lonely out here by yourself."

"Never."

"What do you do?"

"Nothing. As much as possible. Other than that, I drive around, see what there is to see—which isn't much, and that's good too." He shrugged. "I read. I drive into Melville every few weeks to pick up supplies and an occasional book."

He paused, his eyes probing Jacob through the dark. "What about you? A Blinder who can see—you're a walking contradiction."

Jacob didn't know how to respond. He felt self-conscious in the firelight.

Xander sensed his discomfort. "Another time," he said. "For now, don't worry. You'll be all right."

"That's what you said yesterday."

For the first time, Xander broke a smile. "You got me."

The flames smoldered. Xander stirred the fire with a stick, collapsing the remains into dull embers. He rose and Jacob followed him through the darkness back to the house, where inside the bright light made Jacob wince. Without a word they retired to their separate rooms. Jacob undressed and crawled into bed, but try as he might, he couldn't sleep. Images of the day's events kept flashing in his mind, tiny fragments that replayed themselves over and over as he stirred within the tangle of sheets. Eventually he drifted off. As he slipped into sleep he imagined a white figure stumbling across the plains as he floated high above, helpless. Whether the figure was Delaney or himself, he wasn't sure.

CHAPTER SIX

He was in the central square. The same music still droned from the loud speakers, the same group of old men still sat hunched together on a bench along the southern wall, saying nothing, waiting for someone to come and take them home. Across the square he saw Egan wander in with several other kids. He recognized them from school, but without hearing their voices, he couldn't remember who was who. For a moment he thought about calling out to Egan, but his friend's name died in his throat. He watched as the group broke into laughter—probably at some joke of Egan's—and then separated, retiring to their respective tiers just as he and Egan had done almost every day since they'd begun school.

When they were gone he turned and headed north into his own tier, weaving around people in the street. No one paid him any mind. It was just like before. An impulse struck him, and he stopped to make faces at a group of three women walking slowly toward him, their expressions sour as they chewed over a neighborhood rumor. He struggled not to laugh as they passed by, oblivious to his teasing. Turning, he froze at the sight of two men coming in his direction, carrying another on a stretcher between them. As they passed, Jacob recognized the man being carried. It was Tobin Fletcher, the sick neighbor Jacob had witnessed stealing food a couple of weeks ago. Tobin's eyes were open as he lay on his back, his head tilted toward Jacob, unmoving. Jacob felt a chill at the unblinking eyes, and he backed up, suddenly afraid those dead orbs could see him. With a flash Tobin disappeared. In his place lay the skeleton Jacob had encountered in the basin, its tattered clothes fluttering in the breeze. Jacob blinked and Tobin was back.

He turned and ran up the street. He needed to get home. He passed the fountain and cut into his neighborhood. Soon he was on his street, and then before his door. He glanced over to the Fletchers'. Tobin's wife, Penny, was sitting in the doorway, her head buried in her hands.

He went to his door and threw it open. Light streamed in, revealing the interior of the house, and his heart raced at the sight of his mother sitting at the table. Her hair lay loose over her shoulders, not pulled back in its normal ponytail. A breeze picked up behind Jacob, sending the chimes by the door singing, lifting a tuft or two of his mother's hair. She didn't seem to notice.

He looked around as he entered. There was no sign of his father. Pulling out a chair, he sat down across from her. She was holding something in her hands. It was a small cube of metal—his music box. She wound it up, and its little song began unfurling. Jacob winced at the plinking notes. The song was in a different key than the doorway chimes, still ringing in the breeze, creating an awkward dissonance. If it grated on him this much, he could only imagine how it must sound to his mother, blessed as she was with perfect pitch. But she didn't seem to notice.

"They let you go, I guess," she said, lifting her head.

"They didn't keep you long. I'm glad."

"What?" Jacob said, confused. Who did she think he was? "It's me. Nobody let me go. I came back on my own. I wanted to see you."

Worry crept across her face. "I don't know who you are," she said. "But you'd better leave. My husband will be home soon."

"Ma!" he shouted, banging the table, so that she started. "It's me, Jacob. Don't you recognize my voice?" He could feel the tears gathering in his eyes.

"Jacob?" she whispered. She shook her head. "He told me you were—"

The chimes suddenly stopped. A shadow came over the room. Jacob turned toward the doorway where Delaney's father stood, one hand on the open door.

Jacob jumped up from the table and leapt for the door as it began to shut. He slammed against it just as it closed, smothering the room with darkness. He began banging on the door, crying to be let out.

Now he realized he could see his hands, ever so faintly, as the slightest glimmer from behind him grew, casting a red glow about the room, illuminating the door before him. Heat licked against the back of his neck. His nostrils flared at the scent of smoke. He whirled around—she was there.

"Delaney!" he cried out, stepping toward the figure.

Once more there was fire in her eyes, only now it began to grow, stretching out tendrils of flame that crept toward him. He withdrew, pulling away from the unbearable heat until his back was against the door, but the burning snakes whipped forward and wrapped around his wrists. They began dragging him toward her, into her outstretched arms, and he screamed for her to stop, screamed her name over and over, hoping she would hear him and have mercy, but she had none. He reached out as she drew him in, clasped his hands around her throat and squeezed, but he had no strength left in him, nothing to make the burning stop.

Jacob sat up in bed, gasping for breath. His heart was racing. He could hear it pounding in his ears, could feel the sweat along his brow. He turned to sit on the edge of the bed and looked down at the patch of sunlight shining on the floor at his feet. That dream—it just wouldn't let him go. No, it wasn't the same. It was a different dream. But the ending was nearly the same, as was the lucidity. He pushed the hair back from his eyes and sighed. He had never had dreams that felt so real before. When he closed his eyes, he could still see his mother. The memory was worth the pain.

He dressed and went downstairs. Xander wasn't there. There was fruit on the table and some rolls. *He must be outside*, Jacob thought, and sat down to eat. He finished breakfast and still the house remained silent. After putting the leftover food away in the refrigerator and clearing the table, he went out onto the deck and looked over the railing. The cruiser was gone. He hadn't heard it leave. Xander must have taken off while Jacob was dreaming.

He looked out at the view. The shadows were long—it was early. The sun was small and white behind him in the east, and the pink moon still shone on the western horizon, a fat crescent hanging above the city.

From where he was, he could see the far-off towers gleam as they caught the morning light. Hopefully Xander would be back soon. It was painful to see his goal before him in the

58

distance, calling to him, waiting for him. He wanted to get to the city as soon as possible. He didn't even care about the Seers anymore. Who knew if he could have a life with them? After yesterday, he was starting to have his doubts. All that mattered was finding Delaney. It was the only thing left that was keeping him going.

He went back inside, settled into an armchair, and waited, watching through the windows for Xander's cruiser to come growling out of the trees and into the yard. An hour passed, then another, and Xander didn't come. Jacob rose now and then to stretch his legs. On occasion he took down a book, scanning the mysterious symbols, wondering what stories they told. He didn't dare poke around too much in case the man came home to find him snooping. Noon came. He took some leftovers from last night out of the refrigerator and ate lunch.

After he finished, he went to the window again. Still no Xander.

He fell back into the armchair and sighed. Maybe he should leave, strike out for the city now. He wouldn't reach it until at least tomorrow, but what difference did another night or two sleeping under the stars make? As for food, he figured he could take some from Xander. The man had already been generous in feeding him. Jacob couldn't imagine he'd mind him borrowing more. In fact, he still had some of those dry bars left—he could just rely on that if he had to. It seemed as if he was wasting time sitting here. Besides, how did he know Xander would even bring him to the city? In spite of yesterday, the man had been reluctant to help him before. All in all, he didn't know what to think of Xander. He couldn't even tell if the man really wanted him here or, if he did, for how long.

All he knew was that Xander lived alone in the middle of nowhere, was moody, and used to kill people. It didn't strike Jacob as a good combination.

A part of him, though, hated to go. The man *had* saved him, had shown some kindness. It was comfortable here, and it felt safe. Wouldn't it be rude to leave without at least thanking him?

Unable to make up his mind, he lingered for the remainder of the day, waiting for his host to return. Around sunset it suddenly occurred to him—he'd forgotten his morning ritual. Happy at least to have something to do, he retrieved the finder from the pack in his room and went out onto the deck. He watched the sun descend behind the city's towers. She had to be there. He knew she was—he felt it. He had followed her this far, and the finder didn't lie. On the other hand, what truth did it tell? He reached into his pocket and felt the weighty metal of the sounder he'd found yesterday clinging to the skeleton's shirt.

Pressing the button on the finder, he took a deep breath and then spoke her name. There it was, the reassuring beep. But something wasn't quite right. The tone was too low. He rotated away from the city and, to his shock, the pulse picked up. It took him all the way around in the opposite direction before it peaked. The house was before him with the hill behind it. Beyond both was where he'd come from. He must have passed her, he realized with a sinking feeling. Somewhere during the ride from the lake to this house, he went by her. He rushed off the deck and scrambled up the hillside behind the house. Reaching the crest, he took another reading.

Now he was totally confused. This time the finder pointed

west, back toward the city. So she was there after all. How could that be? *It must be broken*, he thought, heading back down the hill. The sinking feeling grew. How could he trust it from now on? Then it suddenly occurred to him—what if it had been broken to start with? What if he had been following a ghost the whole time? What if he'd left Harmony for nothing? Worst of all, what if Delaney had been dead all along?

He stumbled onto the deck. Almost completely numb now, he decided to try one last time. To his chagrin, the finder again pointed east. He closed his eyes. Then it really was broken. Unless . . . His eyes snapped open, settling on the house in front of him.

He ran inside and turned all about, his excitement growing as the finder fluctuated wildly. He raised it above him, and the pulse quickened as the finder pointed toward the upstairs. He climbed the stairs, gripping the banister tightly, listening as the tone swelled with every step. He reached the top and made his way along the balcony. The finder led him to a door. It led him to Xander's closed door.

Forgetting his earlier shyness about snooping, he opened the door and went in, his heart pounding. As he approached the bed a noise made him stop. He turned the finder off and listened. It was a note. No, it was two pitches, a chord of two sounders coming within range of each other. One pitch he hadn't heard before—it came from his pocket. He pulled the sounder he'd taken from the body out and held it in the palm of his hand. Sure enough, its tone rang strong. But that wasn't the sound that caught him, that made his hand shake as he moved closer to the nightstand. It was the other pitch, the other note—it was her sound. Tapping the sounder in his hand silent, he opened the nightstand drawer and removed

61

the singing piece of silver. There was no mistaking the note he'd heard so many times before. It was Delaney's sounder.

He turned it off and sat down on the edge of the bed. His head was spinning. A sudden image rose within his mind's eye—the sight of Xander cutting through the tall grass, before bending down to touch the body perfect in its stillness, to tear the metal disk from its tunic, from her tattered tunic.

The image faded, replaced by another which made his heart beat harder. This time, Xander was climbing the steps to his house, escorting the figure of a girl, that same grim smile on his face that Jacob had seen yesterday at the lake, leading her into a house she would never leave.

He had to go, escape while he still could.

He jumped up and ran out into the hall, then froze at the top of the stairs. If he left now, he'd never know what happened to Delaney. Then where would he go? What purpose would he have? The man knew nothing of his discovery or of his connection with Delaney aside from their shared birthplace. He had to stay and somehow find out, play dumb and wait for the moment to strike.

The growling of an engine sounded outside. Xander had returned. Jacob dashed back into the bedroom, closed the drawer, and left, careful to shut the door behind him. He kept Delaney's sounder, though, making a vow never to lose it. He went down the hall to his own room and crawled into bed, burying himself beneath the covers.

A moment later, Jacob heard Xander come into the house. His bedroom door was closed, and for a minute, there was no sound from below. Then he heard the stairs creak, heard Xander make his way down the balcony hall to his door. He buried his face in the pillow as the door behind him creaked open, hoping the blankets were thick enough to muffle his pounding heart. To his relief the door closed again, though he didn't resume breathing until Xander had gone back down the stairs.

Jacob crept through the trees toward the light. From time to time he could catch glimpses of the flames, hear the crackle of the fire as he closed in, drawn by the smell of smoke. Gripping the long kitchen knife he'd swiped from the house, he took slow, cautious steps, careful to avoid a cracking twig or upturned root. Soon, he was close enough to see him. Xander's back was to Jacob, a dark profile silhouetted by the fire.

Jacob was at the edge of the clearing now. *Almost there*, he thought.

He had waited over an hour in bed, listening to Xander as he made supper, ate, and then cleaned up. The whole time Jacob tried to think of what to do, how to confront the man. How could a boy like him force the truth from someone like Xander? Then it was quiet below. Jacob waited a while before slinking to the door and opening it a crack. Nothing stirred. Slipping downstairs, he opened the deck door to confirm his suspicion. Sure enough, the fragrant smoke of zephyr wood lingered in the air. He grabbed the only weapon he could find from the kitchen and headed out into the dark. He didn't know if this would work, but he would do his best to make the man talk. One way or another, he would find out what had become of Delaney.

Now, as Xander pitched a small log into the fire, Jacob debated how to cross this last stretch of open terrain. Make a run for it and get the point of his knife up against the back of

Xander's neck before the man could react, or continue his silent creep? So far, Xander hadn't looked around or shown he had any idea he was being stalked. Jacob decided to opt for quiet.

Taking a deep breath, he stepped out of the shadows and started toward the figure with slow steps. The knife hovered before him, occupying the space between himself and Xander, seeming to fill it. He was close now. He reached out with the knife, readying the words of confrontation he'd been practicing over and over again for the last hour.

It was as if he were moving in slow motion, or even frozen in place, compared with the man who, without a word, turned and reached out silently with one arm, grabbing the wrist of Jacob's knife-wielding hand. He could do nothing but watch as the man pulled him in, relieved him of his knife, and flipped him over onto his back in one motion. Time resumed its normal pace as he hit the ground, grunting with impact. He was pinned, with Xander on top, looking down with what certainly wasn't surprise but perhaps the slightest bit of amusement. The flames cast shadows that danced across his face.

"Not bad, Blinder. But you're going to have to move quieter than that if you want to surprise me from behind."

Jacob cried out, struggling to free his arms, trying to get at least a kicking foot free, but Xander had him firmly restrained. *This is it*, he thought.

"I knew you weren't sleeping," the soldier said, shaking his head.

"What did you do to her?" Jacob shouted. If he was going to die, at least he'd know the truth.

"Who?" the man demanded.

"You know!"

Xander frowned. He rose, lifting Jacob with him off the ground, and placed him, panting, on his seat. He sat down across the fire on a rock.

"She's fine," he murmured. "At least she was when I left her." He looked up at Jacob. "How'd you know?" he asked. Jacob took the silver whorl from his pocket. It glinted in the firelight. Xander's eyes narrowed.

Jacob didn't feel like explaining. "Just tell me what happened to Delaney."

Xander sighed. "It was a few weeks ago. Two, three, I don't remember. I picked her up on the plains maybe ten miles east of where we met—a Blinder like you, only this girl really was blind. She was in terrible shape—dehydrated, hadn't eaten in days, cuts and bruises all over her. I noticed this flash of white clothing on top of a rise, and it turned out to be her. She didn't say much at first. She was scared of me. I figured she was lost, offered to take her back to Harmony, but she begged me not to. Kept asking that I take her to the city. Insisted on it."

"So what did you do?"

"I did what she asked," Xander said with a shrug. "I drove her to Melville. Wasn't sure what to do with her, so I brought her to Mixel. They said they'd take care of her. I haven't been back yet, so I don't know what happened."

"How'd you end up with this?" Jacob asked, holding out the sounder.

"She gave it to me as a gift when we parted. Said she wouldn't need it anymore. Said she didn't want it."

Jacob shook his head. A part of him was elated to know Delaney had survived. But the joy was tinged with dismay, even resentment, toward her rescuer. "Why didn't you tell me any of this before?"

Xander picked up a chunk of wood and flung it into the fire, sending up a shower of sparks. "Look, Jacob," he said at last, "to be honest, I didn't really want to get involved in all of this—saving her, saving you. That's not what I came out here for."

"Then why did you?" Jacob asked. Xander looked away without answering.

They were silent for a long time. The fire began to burn down.

"I heard you calling out her name last night in your sleep," Xander said, breaking the quiet.

"They told us she was dead," Jacob whispered. "But I knew it wasn't true."

"So you two were friends, huh?"

Jacob wasn't sure how to answer. All that kept flashing through his mind was the memory of the last time he had been with her, on the hill during the delivery, the sadness in her voice, the way in which she had held his hand, pleading.

"My mother's a musician and Delaney was her apprentice. She was at our house almost every day. She was practically a sister—always nice to me, but sad too, and restless. It wasn't until the end that I realized how much she was struggling, as if she was lost. I didn't know how to help her."

"Some people are just lost souls. Isn't much you can do for them—they have to figure it out for themselves. Kind of like you."

"Thanks," Jacob said.

"Well, that's how it seems. I mean, why did you leave, anyway?" Xander asked, placing another log on the fire.

"I told you who I am—or who I was—now it's your turn."

As the fire burned and sparks drifted up into the night, Jacob recounted the story. He told Xander about the movement into sight, about everything he had seen, and about being led to the ghostbox for correction. The man listened quietly the entire time, watching in the glow of firelight. When Jacob finished, Xander remained silent for several minutes before speaking.

"That's quite a story. I thought the army was strict, but your people have us beat by a mile, at least when it comes to discipline and loyalty."

"What do you know about Harmony?" Jacob snapped. The defensiveness in his voice surprised him. Xander nodded.

"See what I mean? After everything that happened, you're still sticking up for them. That's loyalty," he replied. He poked at the glowing embers with a stick, then continued. "Oh, I know about your home. Every once in a while I end up there while I'm driving around. I don't get too close, but I watch through the scopes from my perch on the western ridge, watch the people working in the fields and walking along the streets. Never stay long. Gets old pretty fast—like watching a colony of ants, everyone going through the motions. Place is kind of dreary, if you ask me. 'Course, I guess that doesn't matter if you're blind."

"It's not that bad, you know. I was pretty happy until . . ." He knew the words but didn't want to say them.

"Until you began to see? Until you began to see for yourself the kind of place you were living in?"

"I guess." Jacob paused. "You don't seem to like my people very much," he said in a strained voice.

"*Your* people, huh?" he snorted. "I don't dislike them, Jacob. I don't even really know them. I suppose I know you, and you're not so bad. Actually, in a way, they interest me—they're dedicated, you have to give them that. And maybe they're not even that different from everyone else. People are always searching for the perfect place away from all the garbage out there in the universe. Sometimes they'll go pretty far and do extreme things to get there." He paused, taking time to select his words before continuing. "But I don't respect the Blinders, Jacob. They're about rejection, about running away from the truth. You can't cut yourself off from the pain of the world." He paused. "It doesn't work," he finally said.

They both stared into the fire in silence for a few moments. Then Jacob said, "Those last few days were horrible, and every time I remember them, all I can picture are those strange faces in the crowd at the last Gathering. Their eyes are open, but they don't see me. I don't like the feeling that leaves me with. It's not right."

"Tell me something—is there *anything* you really miss about Harmony?" Xander asked.

"I miss knowing my place in the world, the feeling that I belonged to something, though I guess I lost that even before I left Harmony," he said, then paused. "My family—I miss my mom and dad. I never got to say good-bye. I used to think they were perfect, just like Harmony; my mother was talented, my father was strong. Near the end I got to see that they weren't so perfect, that maybe they weren't even happy. What's funny is that it makes me miss them even more."

"Family is like that," Xander said.

"What about you? Do you have a family?"

Xander stirred the fire with the blackened end of his stick, collapsing the glowing chunks of logs into embers. "It's getting late—I've got a lot to do tomorrow. I'm going to bed," he said, rising. He broke the stick across his knee and threw both pieces into the pit before disappearing into the darkness.

Jacob didn't follow him. For another hour he fed the fire twigs, watching each one ignite quickly, flare into brief and sudden light, then disappear into the bed of coals that brought the next to flames.

CHAPTER SEVEN

That night, Jacob could hardly sleep. All he could do was lie in bed and think about Delaney. The next morning, he asked Xander if they could make the journey to Melville to find her.

"Not unless you want to walk," Xander replied.

"Please, Xander," he begged. "I have to see her."

It was true. The thought of finding Delaney, of being able to actually see her face and hear her voice, was what had kept him going in his march across the plains, was what had given him the strength to leave Harmony in the first place. The idea that a person he loved, a person he had once thought dead, was out there right now, alive and waiting, was too much to bear. But there was something else that made him so eager to find her.

Lying in bed last night, in this strange house, he began to think more about his own future. Xander had said he could stay here, but the invitation wasn't open-ended. After this, where would he go? Back in Harmony, Jacob had been nervously awaiting the day when the council would assign him his role in the community. He'd been so anxious about what his place would be. Then along came his sight, driving out all thoughts of the future. Now his anxiety had returned, but with it came a hope. If he could be reunited with Delaney, he wouldn't be alone, he would have a place in the world. He could face the future with someone who shared his past.

Not only that, there was the matter of the dreams. He'd returned to the same dream last night—chasing the same fluttering white figure through the streets of Harmony, freezing in the face of her flaming eyes, screaming as the burning tendrils of fire entwined him. Somehow he felt that if he could only see the real Delaney, then maybe he could put an end to the nightly torment.

Now, seeing the hesitation on Xander's face, an idea came to mind.

"Just think," he offered, "if you bring me to Melville, then you can get rid of me. I can stay with Delaney."

Xander snorted at the proposal, but nodded at last. "I have to go to Melville next week," he murmured. "We'll be right near Mixel headquarters anyway."

"Thank you, Xander!"

"Don't get too excited, Blinder," the man hastened to add. "Who knows if she's still even there. Like I said last night—I just dropped her off. I don't know what they decided to do with her. For all we know, she might be back in Harmony."

"She isn't," Jacob said, shaking his head. "She wanted to leave so badly. She would never go back, I'm sure of it. You don't know how Delaney is when she gets something in her mind."

Xander grunted. "I'm starting to get an idea," he said.

The rest of Jacob's week was a slow torture of waiting. For the most part Xander kept to himself. He asked Jacob no more questions about his past. Some days he didn't say much at all. Jacob struggled at first to read his mood. At times the man

71

seemed friendly, easygoing. Other times he was taciturn, consumed with bitterness, then he'd climb into his cruiser and take off, only to return hours later in better spirits, sometimes with a load of wood he'd gathered. Often he'd sit in his chair and gaze out the window or read a book, and sometimes Jacob would sit beside him in the other chair and neither of them would speak. Xander seemed to appreciate Jacob's respect for silence, and in turn, Jacob enjoyed the temporary serenity that had been missing from his recent life.

Though Xander had his moments, as the week went on Jacob could feel him change. While he still remained closed about his past, he became chattier, seemed more relaxed with the idea of having Jacob around. He began taking Jacob for rides in the cruiser, showing him the countryside. They even went back to the lake where Jacob had met the other Seers. Jacob felt nervous walking onto the beach, but Xander assured him that Turner and company were long gone. So were the teens—the beach looked like no one had been back since that afternoon. While Xander waded in, Jacob sat on the sand, refusing the man's offer to teach him how to swim.

Jacob did convince Xander, though, to teach him how to identify the letters in Xander's books. He was fascinated with the concept of reading, with the ability to communicate in silence. The idea that a certain sequence of images could trigger a world of thoughts in one's head with no other voice to color the words appealed to him. Xander was reluctant at first. "It takes a while to learn to read," he said, as if unsure Jacob would be around long enough to be taught, but he agreed to at least show Jacob the sounds of letters.

He also taught Jacob the names of colors, giving him the means to understand the myriad hues that made up the world. Jacob loved learning colors even more than reading, as if being taught their names made each one more brilliant, the world somehow more vivid.

Each night as they meditated before the fire, Jacob resisted asking Xander if tomorrow was the day they would travel to Melville. But as each day came and went it got harder, so that by the night of Jacob's eighth day with Xander, it took every ounce of willpower not to put forth the question. That night, though, as Xander knocked the embers down into their glowing bed, Jacob finally heard the words he'd been waiting for.

"I've got to head into town tomorrow," Xander said. "Still want to go?"

Jacob snapped his eyes up from where they'd been watching the coals. Before he could even answer, the man began laughing. Jacob laughed too, then, riding on the wave of excitement, closed his eyes and tried imagining the moment of his reunion with Delaney. All he could see was the flow of black hair from the girl in his dream.

"What does she look like?" Jacob asked, opening his eyes.

The laughter stopped. Xander's face, red in the embers' light, grew intent.

"She's beautiful," he said.

They started out in the white light of morning. Jacob shielded his ears against the roar of the cruiser as it flew across the plains toward the city. As they traveled the worn path, taking the hills with such speed that the truck seemed to float momentarily at each rise, Xander looked back from time to time at the boy strapped into the backseat and grinned, his teeth flashing between lips curled back in amusement at his passenger's blanched complexion. Even though Jacob had ridden in the cruiser several times, he still wasn't completely used to the sensation. He tried to smile back, to show him that he wasn't afraid, and after a while he wasn't anymore, as his body relaxed to the vibrating rhythms of the machine.

The drive took longer than Jacob expected; it was nearly two hours before they reached Melville. As they crested each ridge Jacob could see the city rise, but for a long while it didn't seem to be growing any larger. Near the end, however, it began to loom before them, and he marveled at the towers rising into the sky, with one near the center of the city standing tall above the others, its black surface gleaming in the sun, bright in spite of its ebony shell. As they approached, the plains began to flatten, and near the city they passed several small neighborhoods that appeared to be mostly comprised of warehouses and repair shops. Seeing the low, square structures reminded Jacob of the storage houses in Harmony, and he wondered if the same people had built them.

Aside from these clusters Melville was remarkably contained. It seemed as if one moment they were whipping through the grass, and the next they were cruising down smooth streets, surrounded by glass buildings of countless shapes and sizes. Small craft like the ones Jacob had seen at the lake skittered above them at different heights among the towers, while at street level other vehicles meandered along the avenues between crowds of people on the sidewalks. Some of the groundcraft sported wheels, like Xander's—though none looked as battered—while others floated on an invisible cushion.

Jacob couldn't stop staring left and right as they moved deeper into the city. The buildings dazzled him. Light was

74

everywhere. Many of the buildings' walls were moving displays of color, a multitude of people, animals, and strange landscapes mixed with writing that he could not yet read. Other glass towers reflected the light of the sky or the images displayed on the buildings across the street, creating a strange symmetry of light, a kaleidoscope of blurring shapes and tinctures. Xander had the cruiser's windows open, allowing the sounds and smells around them to drift in. Combined with colors and movement, the panorama overwhelmed Jacob, flooding his senses, leaving him dizzy from the stimulation. He asked Xander to stop for a moment, and the soldier pulled over near the sidewalk.

"You all right?" Xander asked, turning around.

"So many people. And the sounds," Jacob said. The air resonated with the buzzing of the craft above them, and loud music poured from a shopping center next to them, the thumping of its heavy bass clutching at Jacob's chest as he watched customers streaming in and out of the building's open doors. The crowd revealed a variety of different-colored clothes and complexions, from the dark tones of Xander to the paleness of his mother.

"It's beautiful," Jacob said. "So bright."

"Don't let it fool you," Xander said. "Melville looks shiny on the surface, but it's got a dirty underside like every other city. The corporation just does a better job at keeping it hidden."

Jacob barely heard him. "Why don't you live here?" he asked.

Xander shrugged his shoulders. "Doesn't do much for me," Xander said, "but I grew up in it. Not on this planet, but one city's the same as the next. Same stores, same companies, same people, just different names, that's all, and sometimes even the names are the same."

Looking around, he shook his head.

"Believe me, you'd soon get used to it until you'd almost forgotten what quiet was like. Anyway, we have business to take care of. I've got to pick up some supplies, and you've got to find your friend."

"Where do we go to do that?" Jacob asked.

"You saw that big black tower on the way in? That's Mixel's headquarters. That's where we're headed. I brought Delaney there too. But before we do any of that, we'll grab lunch. And you need new clothes."

Glancing at his frayed tunic and grass-stained trousers, Jacob's face reddened. He'd been wearing these same clothes almost every day for the last six months and was so accustomed to the coarse garments that he hadn't noticed until reaching the Seers just how ragged he was.

"We can go in there." Xander pointed, exiting the cruiser and helping Jacob onto the sidewalk.

They passed through an entrance rimmed with flashing lights into a mall. Before long, they'd entered a store that Jacob could have sworn was as big as Harmony itself and made their way to the clothing section. Xander stood by with an amused look as two young women assisted Jacob, twittering to each other when they saw him. They had him remove his old clothes, which they discarded—handling them with obvious distaste—and soon had him dressed in lightweight pants accompanied by a shirt made of a fabric that alternated between shades of blue as he moved under the bright lights in the ceiling. The close-fitting garments felt odd against his skin, but he enjoyed the freedom of movement they provided compared to his old, baggy smock. They gave him a new jacket and a pair of light boots that Xander selected for him.

"You need these where we live," he said. Jacob found it both strange and somehow comforting that Xander had used the word "we."

The girls whisked him to another section of the store, where several men and women were cutting and styling customers' hair. They had him recline in a chair so that his hair could be washed and then an older woman gave him a trim. As she snipped away, twittering to another hairdresser nearby, Jacob closed his eyes and imagined his mother's face, imagined that the stranger's fingers gently parting the strands of his hair were hers. He had always taken comfort in the closeness, the quiet, of the ritual. He could almost hear her voice, humming to the rhythm of the shears.

"Almost finished," the woman said, rousing him from memory.

When everything was completed, they hurried him back to the clothing section and stood him before a full-length mirror. He gazed at his reflection in amazement. The mirror revealed a different person from the one he had seen in the pool at the grove on the plains, though the eyes remained the same. Wide-eyed, he turned to Xander, who merely nodded.

"You clean up pretty good, Blinder."

A short while later, they were heading toward Mixel Tower. Xander drove his cruiser right up front, gunning the throttle before cutting the ignition. Its loud engine drew stares from the people passing in and out of the revolving doors at the base of the giant high-rise.

"Don't mind the suits," Xander said as they passed through the spinning glass portal. "Let 'em stare. I like to

77

remind them that it's people like me who helped secure their brilliant futures."

Jacob followed him into the vast lobby of the tower. As they cut through the crowd toward the elevator shafts, Jacob looked around in awe. An enormous video screen, at least twenty feet wide, sat like a noble perched on a throne above them, silent, displaying a steady stream of stock prices superimposed on fragments of news stories broadcast from across space. The glowing screen cast dull and hazy beams of color that danced in the dark hall, while the footfalls and murmurs of the crowd echoed in the high, vaulted ceiling. Jacob breathed a sigh of relief when they entered the bright enclosure of the lift and the doors closed with a hiss.

They rode the elevator only a few seconds before it came to a sudden stop. The doors opened and Xander exited with his usual rapid stride, straight and determined, so that Jacob had to trot to keep up. They walked down a hallway before turning into an office that contained a waiting area with chairs and a counter up front. Behind it sat a young man with short black hair. He gazed unblinking as Xander approached. For a moment the two stared at each other.

"Hello?" Xander said, waving a hand in front of the man's face. The man started slightly, but his facial expression remained unchanged.

"Yes?" the man replied.

"I was here a few weeks ago . . . ?"

"I'm sorry, I don't remember."

Xander sighed. "Merc 32476."

Jacob watched the man punch the numbers into a machine before him.

"Yes, Mr. Payne," the man said. "What can I do for you?"

78

"I brought a girl in last time I was here. Remember now?"

The man's eyebrows rose, and he nodded in recognition. "That's right. Of course. The beautiful, mysterious Delaney. She's become quite popular with the board lately. A real find."

"Then she's still around? The kid here is a friend of hers and he'd like to visit her. Where is she staying?"

"Well, right upstairs, Suite 767, but I don't think—"

Xander turned and headed toward the door with Jacob trailing behind him.

"Mr. Payne, wait!" the young man cried.

"Thanks for the help!" Xander shouted as he left the office and headed to the elevator.

The elevator zipped them to the seventy-sixth floor. A few moments later they stood in the silent hallway before the door of her suite. Jacob looked nervously at Xander, who motioned toward the door with an upturned hand. Jacob knocked quietly at first, and then louder. The door opened but no one appeared. When Jacob hesitated, Xander prodded him and they entered the small hallway, the door whispering shut behind them.

They turned into a room illuminated by an enormous pane of glass along the far wall. A grand piano occupied the center of the apartment. In a chair near the window sat a young woman, her back to them. Her raven hair—the same color and sheen as the piano—cascaded down over her shoulders and over her white gown.

A prickling sensation rose along the back of Jacob's neck and his heart began to pound. For a moment, he thought he was stuck back in the nightly world of his dream. There was something eerily familiar about seeing the figure from behind. The sound of her voice snapped him back.

"It's not time yet. Go away," she said. Jacob trembled at the unmistakable timbre of Delaney's voice.

The girl rose and faced them. Jacob stared in amazement at her shimmering robes and at the delicate beauty of her face. But what froze him in place, what both captivated and terrified him, were her eyes.

Her human eyes were gone. In their place sparkled almond-shaped crystal orbs. Rimmed by a thin line of gold that stretched from the corners, along the temples, and into the hairline, the unblinking eyes seemed to glow with a fire of their own.

CHAPTER EIGHT

For what seemed like a long time Jacob could only stare at
those eyes, too shocked to speak. Aside from the strangeness
of seeing Delaney for the first time, he was bombarded with
the sensation of being back in his dream. The room was
bright, but he half expected it to go black, to have the world
reduced to that now familiar tunnel with just himself and
Delaney, to see the fire erupt from her eyes. He had thought
their reuniting would be a moment of happiness, but instead
he was confused, distracted.

"Who are you?" Delaney at last demanded, brusquely
trying to mask her fear.

"It's me, Jacob," he said. His voice sounded small in his
ears, far away.

"Jacob?" she whispered. "Is it really you?"

She rushed over and threw her arms around him.
Trembling, she sat on a couch and pulled him down next to
her.

"Jacob, you have no idea how wonderful it is to hear a
familiar voice. What are you doing here, anyway? And your
eyes—they're following me. Can you see?"

"Yes," Jacob said. "I don't know why, but I began to see—
right after you left. That's why I had to leave Harmony." He

shook his head. "It's a long story."

"I'm just glad you're here," she said. Once again, she pulled him close and held him, as if she would never let him go. Jacob remembered the morning of his last birthday just weeks ago, how his mother had held him the same way before he left her to play in the sun.

She looked over at Xander. "Who's this with you? Did he bring you here?" she asked.

"This is Xander," Jacob said as the man came forward from where he lingered at the edge of the room.

"That's right," Xander said. "I brought him here, just like I brought you."

She started. "I know you. You wanted to take me back to Harmony, but I made you bring me here . . ." Her voice trailed off.

"What happened to your eyes, Delaney?" Jacob asked.

"Do you like them?" she said with a quick, high laugh. "They're beautiful, aren't they? Very expensive. You could probably buy our entire colony with them. That's what they told me anyway," she said.

"They just gave them to you?" Xander asked.

"Yes," she said. She sat back and crossed her legs. Her clasped hands balanced on top of her knees. "They've given me everything. New eyes, a new life. Anything I ask for, they'll get it. Do you like this place, Jacob? Come look out the window."

She took his hand and drew him to the expanse of glass. From the seventy-sixth floor of Mixel Tower the city of Melville appeared small and defined, stretching below like a disc with sharp edges marking where the city ended and the plains began. A few structures rose from the symmetrical grid work, but even the tallest of them was only half the height of the tower that was the hub of this colonial city.

"I could stare out this window for hours," she said. "Seeing is so incredible. Better than I ever imagined. It's like . . . well, you know what's it like, don't you, Jacob."

"Yes," he said.

It was early afternoon. Even beneath the sun, the city seemed to burn with a light of its own. From here the people in the street were specks. Even the ground cars and low-flying floaters were meager dots. From time to time a floater would buzz by, climbing to Mixel Tower's roof or dropping back into the grid below. The only nearby object of any size was a rising ship, its engine burners flaring as it drifted from the spaceport on its way to orbit or beyond.

"The world looks small from up here, doesn't it?" she said.

"It depends on where you're looking," Jacob replied.

Moving his eyes upward, he gazed at the eastern horizon. After the city dropped off, all that remained were hills of grass, low and indistinct. Row after row stretched out, punctuated here and there with the small, irregular shapes of lakes and ponds glittering in the afternoon sun. From here it seemed hard to believe he'd walked all that distance over the land. How far was it anyway? Somewhere buried in the plains beyond the horizon was Harmony, alone, cut off and oblivious to this humming island of light.

"Harmony's over there," he said, pointing.

"You can't see it," she said. "It's too far away." She turned and left the window. "That's the only thing about this suite— I wish it faced west instead of east. I'm not interested in looking east. The sea is on the western side, just beyond the city. Have you seen the ocean yet, Jacob?"

"No."

"It glimmers. It's dazzling. And there are islands. Hundreds of them. I'm going to get a west-facing room. Jack said he'd move me."

"Who's Jack?" Jacob asked.

"Jack LaPerle. He took me in and gave me my eyes. And more."

"What do you mean?"

She smiled and took his hands, glancing around as if she were about to tell him a precious secret. "I'm a star, Jacob. A celebrity."

"What does *that* mean?"

"I'm famous. Or at least I'm starting to be. Jack says soon everyone will know me. Not just here. People everywhere. People out there," she said, pointing out the window toward the sky.

Jacob tried to smile back. He was having a hard time understanding everything she was saying. He didn't know why, but the whole conversation was going just the opposite of what he'd expected. "What are you famous for?" he asked.

"Music, Jacob. That's what I do now—like in Harmony, only a hundred times as many people hear me, thousands even. Jack says I've got flair. I've got an image that people will go for."

"So what do you do all day?" Jacob asked.

"Well," she said, looking around, "I'm here a lot of the time. I practice a lot. You see the piano I've got—there's nothing like it in Harmony. The sound is amazing. Other than that, I'm pretty busy. A lot of nights, I perform. At first it was for small groups—men who work here, important men, and friends of theirs. And then they had me record. You know,

Jacob, like the recordings we listened to back in Harmony. I have my own. You can hear me singing and playing. And now they're selling them everywhere!"

"Who's selling them?" Xander asked.

"I don't know," she said. "Mixel, I guess."

"Hmph," Xander snorted.

Jacob didn't know what Xander was responding to. He only cared about one thing.

"Just tell me, Delaney—are you happy here?" he asked. "Is this what you want?"

She paused. "Of course it is," she said with a smile. "I am happy, Jacob. Very happy. I have everything I want. I have more than I could've imagined."

She moved to the piano and sat down. The opal keys spread before her, waiting. Her fingers traced along their surface, gently fell to play a single chord, her foot on the damper pedal muting the chord as it hovered before dying.

"Why shouldn't I be?" she said.

As if in answer to the chord, a light tone sounded, followed by the swish of the opening door. Delaney rose from the bench. Jacob and Xander turned as two men entered the room. The one in front was not much taller than Jacob. His slicked-back blond hair and bronzed skin reminded Jacob of the older kids at the lake. The rich fabric of his suit glistened under the light, the metallic sheen fragmenting into the suggestion of a rainbow. The man behind was huge in comparison. His suit, multihued like the other's, barely contained his thick arms and chest.

"I'm sorry," the smaller man in front cooed, his face breaking into a wide grin, "but fans are not allowed into Miss Corrow's quarters. Delaney, I'm sorry for the disturbance.

I simply don't know how they got in here."

"This is Jack LaPerle," Delaney said to Jacob and Xander. "It's okay, Jack. They're friends of mine."

"Friends? I didn't realize you'd made any friends, Delaney. How delightful," he said. Jacob hadn't thought it was possible, but LaPerle's grin seemed to stretch even wider.

"Well, Jacob and I go back," she said.

"That's delightful," he said again. He turned to Jacob and Xander. "We're so lucky that Delaney has decided to join us here at Mixel. I'm sure she's told you all about her success."

"It's just nice to see her," Jacob replied. "I was worried about you, Delaney."

"That's so sweet," LaPerle said before Delaney could answer. "Anyway, Delaney, I feel absolutely terrible about doing this, but, friends or fans, I'm afraid they'll both have to go for now."

"Can't Jacob stay with me?" Delaney asked, coming over behind Jacob and placing her arms around him.

"That's not for the best right now," he replied. "You've got a busy schedule and we need you to be focused."

"Come on, Jack," Delaney said. "I'm tired of spending all my time here alone. It would be good to have some company."

Jacob could hear the edge creeping into her voice. For a moment, it reminded him of how she'd spoken to her father back in Harmony.

"Listen, Jack," Xander interrupted, "this young man's a friend of Delaney's. She isn't a prisoner, is she?"

LaPerle's smile vanished. "No, Mr. Payne, she isn't," he said, seeming to enjoy the look of surprise that flashed over Xander's face at the mention of his name. "But I'm afraid that Miss Corrow is expected at an engagement shortly and must get ready. Perhaps you can visit another time. Mr. Smith will show you out. Karl?" LaPerle turned to the giant behind him. The man gestured to the door.

"Don't worry, we're leaving," Xander snapped. "Come on, Jacob." He turned back to Delaney. "Delaney, it was a pleasure seeing you again."

She managed a smile. "Bye, Jacob. Promise you'll come back soon."

"I promise," Jacob said.

He followed Xander and Karl to the door. Passing LaPerle, he glanced over. The man stared back, a thin smile on his face.

The last thing Jacob saw before leaving was Delaney. Looking behind him, he saw her standing behind LaPerle, one arm raised in farewell, her eyes gleaming points of light. For the briefest moment, Jacob could have sworn he saw those eyes flicker, flare a moment before dulling. Then he was out into the hall, halfway to the elevator before the door had even whispered shut behind them.

CHAPTER NINE

The three of them made their way to the elevator in silence. Jacob walked between the two men, trying to steal glances at both. Xander's momentary anger back in the suite had been replaced with his customary dispassionate look. The giant's face was blank, as well. They reached the elevator and still no one spoke. Jacob felt tense and oddly guilty. He'd done nothing wrong, but the huge man's presence made him feel like a criminal. An image of the two listeners escorting him from school to the council house flashed through his mind. He moved a little closer to Xander.

The door of the elevator opened and the three entered. Again, Jacob was between them, but now the two men faced each other. Jacob shrank against the wall as the pair's faces hardened into a mutual glare. *Hurry up*, Jacob thought, wishing he could boost the speed of the falling elevator. He didn't want to be in this tiny room another second with these two men.

Jacob took a sharp breath as the pair stepped toward each other, their faces now only an inch apart. Before Jacob could say anything, both men broke into a laugh and joined in a rugged, brief embrace.

"Damn, Xander, it's good to see you," Karl said, still gripping Xander's shoulder. Xander lightly slapped the giant's cheek in return.

"Good to see you too," he said.

"You two know each other?" Jacob cried.

"Karl and I," Xander said, pausing, "we worked together."

"Worked together, huh? That's a pretty way of putting it," Karl snorted. "So how are you doing anyway? Haven't seen you in ages. Since you got done, I guess."

"I'm fine, Karl. I'm here on Nova Campi now. Got a little place on the plains."

"No kidding. Doesn't surprise me."

"Yeah, question is—what're you doing here? Don't tell me you like working for that girl's handler."

Karl shrugged. "I work for Mixel, he works for Mixel—that's how that is. It pays well, and it beats risking your neck for God-knows-what."

"I suppose. But that suit. He's the kind we used to hate."

"Come on, Xander, give me a break," Karl said. "Besides, we all have our different ways of dealing, right? Look at you, after all, living in the bush."

Xander's grin faded just as the elevator door opened. Karl gestured toward the lobby. Xander took Jacob by the shoulder and the two of them walked out.

"Xander!" Karl shouted as they started walking away. They turned back to where he stood, holding open the door. "I *am* sorry," he said. "I never got a chance to tell you. I just wanted you to know."

Xander nodded and started to walk away when Karl called out a second time.

"What is it?" Xander asked.

"Better not come back here again. Okay?"

"We'll see," Xander replied.

• • •

Jacob looked back to find Melville's skyscrapers shrunken by distance. Even Mixel Tower had diminished somewhat, though the black monolith still dominated the city's skyline. Plugging his ears to block out the roar of the cruiser, he turned back around. To the left and right the grass was a blur of bluish green, consolidated into a single wave flowing away from him as they ripped across the land. Though the sun still shone behind him in the west, ahead, over Xander's shoulder, he could see the purple moon breaking the surface of the horizon. Its great rings rose at an angle, giving the swollen orb a tilted look, as if some great hand were lifting it by one end. Xander looked back as he had from time to time on the journey in, but now he wasn't smiling. Jacob was glad. He didn't feel like smiling either.

After leaving Mixel, Xander still had to pick up some supplies and Jacob tagged along, trying not to get in his way. The man had fallen into a foul mood, and by now Jacob knew not to say anything that might draw his anger to the surface. Still, he wanted to know what Karl had been talking about. What was he sorry for? And he was troubled by his warning not to come back.

But Karl's comments—and Xander's reaction to them—weren't what really ate at Jacob. He had forgotten them almost entirely by the time they started out from the city as a larger anxiety rose within, like the purple moon before him.

It was Delaney.

Ever since leaving Mixel Tower, a knot in Jacob's stomach had been growing. Nothing had turned out the way he'd hoped. First, to see Delaney so . . . different. And it wasn't just the eyes. Something about her wasn't right. It didn't feel like he was talking to the same person. But what had changed? Maybe it was just because she was happy. He'd been so used to her misery back in Harmony, especially at the very end, that he must have forgotten what it was like to see her happy. Or to see her at all. Maybe that was it. Maybe the shock of seeing this person he'd known for so long in his blindness made it impossible for him not to feel strange at their meeting. He tried to think back to the first moments he saw his mother, his father, his best friend, Egan. Then it was strange too, but that wasn't quite it—there was something else. He closed his eyes, leaned his head back against the vibrating seat, and sighed. Maybe it was *him*—maybe he had changed so much that nothing would ever be the same.

All he knew was that something wasn't right. Delaney claimed she was happy, but he couldn't help wondering if she was faking it. In fact, none of it seemed real—from her eyes, to the suite, to the man she claimed had given her so much.

"I don't like that man," Jacob said later that night. He was leaning against the railing of the deck, having come out after dinner for some air. Xander had joined him and the two now looked out toward Melville. From here it was nothing more than a few meager lights, and even they were nearly drowned by the brightness of the purple moon falling fast before them, dropping toward the city.

"Karl's a good guy," Xander said. "Tough. I can't remember how many times we saved each other's skin."

"Not Karl," Jacob said. "The other one."

"LaPerle? You probably shouldn't like him. Handlers are slick. They're supposed to be."

Jacob thought back to his first encounter with the Seers at the lake. "He looked like Garrett and his friends, but somehow he reminded me of Turner."

Xander snorted. "That's not far off. But I wouldn't worry too much about Delaney. She may be miserable, but I don't think she's in any real danger."

"You don't think she's happy?"

The man shrugged. "You know her. Couldn't you tell?"

"Not really," Jacob said, then hesitated. "Maybe. All I know is that today wasn't good. I wanted it to be good, and it wasn't." He sighed. "I guess I had this idea that she needed me."

"She probably does," Xander offered.

"It didn't seem like it," Jacob murmured. *If she doesn't,* he thought, *then where does that leave me?* "Maybe I just needed her instead," he said.

"Don't worry about it."

"I can't help it. Back in Harmony, all I knew was a sad girl. She didn't fit in. She talked about leaving. I even heard her say she wanted to see. And now she's got that, just like me. Everything that's happened to me has happened to her, just in a different way."

"Do you think she's better off than you?"

"I don't know. I guess. She wanted to leave Harmony. She chose to. I didn't. And now she's a part of something. She has a new family, people who adore her."

Xander sighed. "First of all, Blinder, she may be a part of Mixel, but it isn't as cozy as you might think. They may be taking care of her, but they really only care about one thing—what they can get from her. That's how they are with everyone. I'm not saying it's bad. After all, it goes both ways. But in the end, it's just business to them. Trust me, I've been there. They're getting something from her, and I don't think she even knows it."

"Delaney's pretty smart," Jacob replied.

"Then she may have already figured it out. Or soon will.

The point is, just because she's a part of something, doesn't make her better off. Both of you were part of something back in Harmony and look how that turned out."

"But at least she has a future. I don't even know where I belong, or what's going to happen to me."

"Don't need to, Jacob. Not right now. And who knows what Delaney's future will be. She might need you someday. No one can see what lies ahead."

Jacob closed his eyes and shuddered as he recalled the sensation of déjà vu he'd felt seeing Delaney this afternoon. At least maybe now, having seen her at last and knowing she was all right, the recurring nightmare would stop.

Opening his eyes again, he looked up to see the moon now slipping into the black land, dragged down by its tilted rings. It was night, but the moonset cast a faint glow over everything, aided by the dimmer light of the cratered pink moon now at its zenith above them.

"It's bright out tonight," Jacob said.

"Once your eyes adjust, there's nothing nicer."

Jacob pointed to the horizon. "Why is that moon so much bigger than the one above us?" he asked. "And so fast—it only rose a few hours ago and it's already sinking down."

"You mean Duna?"

"That's what it's called?"

"Yeah. The other's Drake. Well," Xander said. "Duna's not a moon. It's a planet. We're the moon. Nova Campi orbits Duna, just like Drake does. People still call it a moon, though. We like to think of ourselves as the center of things, I guess."

"I didn't know," Jacob said. "They never taught us that. They said there were two moons, but they never told us their names. Maybe *they* didn't know."

"It doesn't really matter. Whatever you call them—whether you even know they're there—they still do what they do. Knowing changes nothing."

Jacob realized on one level Xander was right. But his own ignorance about this basic truth, about this fundamental part of the world in which he lived, bothered him. Still, why should he be surprised? Everything about the world was different from what he'd thought it was.

"Don't worry about Delaney," Xander said. "We'll see her again soon, and things will be better. It was your first trip into the city. You were just overwhelmed by everything today."

"But what if we don't? What if we can't? You heard what Karl said as we were leaving. He may be a friend of yours, but he sounded serious. I might never see her again."

"Don't be foolish, Blinder. Of course you will."

"How?"

"Let me take care of that," Xander replied. He turned to go inside, stopping at the door. "I spent my whole life taking orders," he called back to Jacob. "When I left the army, I promised myself I'd never let anybody tell me what I can or can't do again. Even Mixel. Especially Mixel."

"When do we go?"

"We'll wait awhile. We'll let them forget about us. It won't take long."

It took about a week. Jacob emerged from his familiar nightmare one dawn to find Xander standing over him, a dark shadow in the thin early light.

"You keep calling out her name," the man said.

"I know," Jacob said. "It always wakes me up."

"It wakes me up too. In fact, it creeps me out, the way

94

your voice sounds. What's wrong?"

"Nothing," Jacob murmured. His brain was a murky mix of sleep and fear, and he didn't want to talk. Seeing Delaney had not put an end to the dreams. If anything, they had grown more intense. More real. There were other changes too. Each night new details, a slight shift of when things happened, of what was said. One development in particular disturbed him. The dream had always ended with his hands around her throat, with the two of them face-to-face, though he could never see her visage through the blaze. But the last few nights the finale had altered. It still ended with him choking her, but he now found himself outside himself, standing to the side watching the struggle unfold, zooming in on the hands tightening around the white neck. And then, in this last dream just moments ago, the latest twist—feeling himself shrink the tighter he squeezed, seeing her grow larger and larger until her head loomed over him, her features cold, indifferent, in spite of the blazing from her eyes.

"Nothing's wrong, huh?" Xander said. "All right. But nothing or not, we're doing something about it."

"What do you mean?" Jacob asked.

"Time we paid Delaney another visit," he said.

"But Karl's warning—" Jacob began.

"Like I said before, no one tells me what to do," Xander snapped. He paused. When he spoke again, his voice was softer. "Besides, it seems clear enough. Until you figure this out, you'll have no peace. And neither will I," he added, looking away.

CHAPTER TEN

The city looked the same from a week ago. The same buildings, the same floaters humming between them, the same glowing pictures playing along the surface of the glass. It all became a blur. Looking out the window of the cruiser as they meandered down the avenue with the afternoon flow of traffic, Jacob thought that even the people passing on the sidewalks looked the same—a teeming mass of different colors and styles blending and flowing into a single stream. In some respects, the scene didn't seem much different from the monotony of Harmony. More people, of course, more colorful, even more dynamic, but still imbued with a sense of sameness, a feeling that life had always been this way and always would remain so, a world oblivious to its own history.

But there was one difference from Harmony that caught Jacob right away: the feel of other eyes upon him, strangers' eyes. Xander's beat-up cruiser stood out against the other groundcars around them and drew frequent stares from passersby. Every now and then one of them would look further, beyond the shell of the craft to Jacob inside. Their eyes would find his and the link would pluck them for a moment from the stream. In that brief glimpse he found a host of looks—distaste from time to time, humor, benevolence, mostly curiosity. Then their eyes would turn away and they would fall back into the flow, whisked back into their own lives.

Xander didn't pull up roaring this time before Mixel Tower. He parked a couple streets away, down a side alley.

"Best keep a low profile today," he explained, helping Jacob to the ground.

"You think they know we're coming?"

"I don't think they've thought about us at all. As far as they're concerned, they don't need to. We're nobody. But who knows."

They merged with the entering crowd, let it usher them through the revolving doors and into the lobby. Fingering the metal weight in his pocket, Jacob clung close to Xander as they made their way across the marble floor toward the elevators. He knew Delaney had given her sounder away, had said she didn't want it anymore, but he'd brought it anyway. Maybe she had changed her mind.

In the elevator, Xander leaned down and put his hand on Jacob's shoulder. His grip was tight but didn't hurt.

"You need to breathe, Blinder," he said.

Jacob managed a meager smile. "Somehow I feel more nervous than before."

"You haven't done anything wrong."

"He told us not to come back. I'm just not used to breaking the rules," Jacob replied. "Not on purpose, anyway."

Xander shrugged. "That wasn't a rule. It was a suggestion. Just think about Delaney. What would she do? If things were reversed."

"She'd be here," Jacob said, nodding.

"That's what I thought."

The door whisked open. They turned into the hallway. LaPerle was waiting, wearing the same wide grin from a week ago. Karl stood behind him, his face blank.

"Delaney's friends!" LaPerle crooned, stepping forward to block them. "Hello again."

"Jack," Xander said. He took a few steps forward toward LaPerle, prompting Karl to follow suit.

"It's so nice you came by for a visit," LaPerle said. He raised a hand and Karl froze. "But I'm afraid Delaney isn't here at the moment."

"That's all right," Xander said. "We don't mind waiting."

LaPerle shrugged his shoulders. "She'll be out for the rest of the day. Her schedule is quite packed."

"That's funny," Xander snapped. "I have a hard time imagining you'd be far away from her. After all, she seems to rely on you so much."

"I do what I can," LaPerle said. "You should call ahead next time. Let us know you're coming. I'm sure we could arrange something."

"Right," Xander snorted. He leaned in toward LaPerle and lowered his voice. "Just tell me one thing. How much have you made?"

LaPerle nodded. "Quite a bit," he said. "And it's only just the beginning. Of course, we've invested a great deal in Delaney. Her eyes are state-of-the-art. Shipped in from Earth, a pretty penny. But quite worth it, I'm sure she'd agree. And this life we've given her—it's only fair we ask a little in return, don't you think? She's a part of us, just like you are."

Xander's eyes narrowed. "Nobody owns me. I fulfilled the terms of my contract."

"You did. And quite well, at that. Numerous commendations, a distinguished record, even a tragic past—I read the file. But you're not clear of us yet. There's the matter of your pension, after all. Mixel still pays the bills, right?"

"Are you threatening me?" Xander said. He took another step forward. Jacob reached up and grabbed his arm. LaPerle waved Karl back once more.

"Of course not, Mr. Payne. I'm just trying to point out all the facts. Keep a sense of perspective. Point of view is everything, is it not?"

"Xander, maybe we should go now," Jacob pleaded. He tugged on the soldier's sleeve.

LaPerle looked down at Jacob and the grin returned. "I know you're disappointed, young man. Maybe next time you can see your friend. And then we can all sit down and have a delightful chat. I'd love to hear about how you two know each other."

Jacob took a step closer to Xander, resisting the urge to back away.

"The boy and I found her," Xander broke in. "She spent a couple days with us. Ever since I brought her here he's been bugging me to see her."

"Well, she certainly is worth seeing. Everyone wants to see her. Speaking of which," he said, reaching into his suit jacket. He pulled out a pair of thin cards and held them out. Jacob reached out, took them tentatively, and studied them. They were light and stiff, iridescent under the glow of the recessed lights.

"What are these?" Jacob asked.

LaPerle's eyes narrowed. "Why they're tickets, of course."

He took one of them from Jacob and held it out flat on his palm. A light flashed and there was Delaney, a shining figure hovering above his hand, no more than six inches tall. Jacob's eyes widened at the sight of her rotating form, her hands held forth, a smile on her face, beckoning. LaPerle flipped the card over and the image disappeared. He handed the ticket back to Jacob.

"Tonight. Eight o'clock at the Marlboro."

"Thanks," Jacob murmured.

"It's the least I can do. And like I said, we'll all get together. Soon, of course. After all, who knows how long she'll be around?"

"What do you mean?" Jacob asked, startled.

"Delaney's on the verge of a breakout. She's already doing well on the Rim. And when the Core worlds pick her up, she's going straight to Earth. Mixel's putting some serious money out there to promote her. It's only a matter of time." He chuckled and shook his head. "It's the eyes," he said. "Everyone loves them. She looks like an Egyptian princess, a goddess."

"Oh," Jacob replied. He didn't know what else to say. He looked down at the floor and tried focusing on the swirled pattern of the carpet.

"Come on, Jacob," Xander said. He turned Jacob around and led him to the elevator. "Thanks for the tickets," he called back. LaPerle and Karl remained watching in the hall, waiting until the elevator came. Jacob hardly noticed when the door opened and Xander ushered him inside.

"That was strange," Jacob said once they were out on the street. "LaPerle and Karl, it's like they were waiting for us."

"They were," Xander replied. "Building's sensors must be keyed into us. LaPerle knew we were coming the moment we walked through the front door."

"I'm just mad we missed her."

"She was there. That bastard was lying," Xander said. "But don't worry. You'll get to see Delaney again."

"So what," Jacob cried. "You heard what that man said. They're going to take her away for good. Even if I see her tomorrow, what does it matter?"

"Don't look at it that way," Xander warned. "If she leaves, she leaves. You can't control what happens to her. Just think— if you'd never gotten your sight, if you'd never left Harmony, you'd still think she was dead right now. This way, at least you know she's alive and that she's going to be fine. Hell, she'll be better off than ninety-five percent of the people out there, including us. That's got to be enough."

It wasn't. Jacob knew that Xander was right on one level, but he couldn't accept it any more than he had been able to accept her death back in Harmony.

They crossed the street and headed down the wide boulevard toward the center of Melville, leaving the cruiser parked in the alley. The Marlboro—a large concert hall—wasn't far away, and they could easily walk back after the show.

"I'm not even sure I feel like going," Jacob mumbled, giving the tickets to Xander.

"I'm not much for concerts myself," he replied, putting the tickets in his shirt pocket. "But we should go. Who knows, maybe you'll be able to see her there. In the meantime, we've got a few hours to kill. Let's walk."

They wandered into a section of the city they'd passed earlier. Jacob recognized the shopping center where last

101

week he'd received his new clothes and haircut. He remembered the anticipation he'd felt that morning as they prepared to find Delaney. All that was gone, replaced by a fear that, once again, he'd have to resign himself to losing her.

They passed the entrance to the plaza, passed the flashing neon colors and ratcheting drumbeats raining down from the speakers above the doors, and continued on past a range of other stores. It was late in the afternoon and the earlier crowds had dwindled. Jacob was glad—even from the removed comfort of the cruiser he'd felt claustrophobic watching the mass of people flow along the street.

Gazing at all the signs, Jacob wished he could read. Though he still wasn't used to this loud alien world of people, color, and glass, he felt even more a stranger, more cut off because of his inability to understand the glowing letters above the stores and in the projected murals along the buildings. He looked across the street at one tower where the glass windows shimmered for a moment, only to be replaced by a black, star-filled sky. Through the ether came a starship, a knobby oval whose burning wake carried a line of words. Jacob was about to ask Xander what they said, when the man took his arm and turned abruptly off the boulevard into a narrow side street.

"Where are we going?" Jacob asked.

"A little place I know. You'll see."

There were no flashing displays in this alley, and the tall building rising over them on both sides cast a shadow over everything. The sky was a narrow line of light. The only other illumination came from the main street's brilliance behind them and a small lamp above the door of a shop about twenty yards away on the right. The rest of the building's face was featureless, making the storefront seem out of place, as if put there by mistake.

Jacob trailed Xander to the entrance, starting at the tinkle of bells when Xander opened the door. Xander went in and Jacob followed, closing the door behind him.

The first thing Jacob noticed was the smell. It was the tiniest bit musty, just mild enough to be pleasant, a dry smell, like withered herbs that still held the memory of sunlight. The odor was followed by the sight of books, row upon row of them stacked against walls and along the shelves that formed aisles within the confines of the tiny shop amid the dimmed lamps. It was cool inside and quiet, and Jacob took a deep breath and touched his ears for a moment in wonder at the silence.

"Xander!" a voice called out. Jacob turned to see a woman appear around an aisle. His eyes widened as she came toward them. He guessed her to be about as old as his mother but her opposite, a negative image. Instead of his mother's pale skin and hair, this woman had short jet-black hair and tight-fitting clothes covering skin that, as she strode beneath a hovering lamp, Jacob realized was a deep shade of purple. Most star- tling of all were her eyes. Her irises were gold, sparkling against the darkness of her face. Looking at them, Jacob couldn't help but think of Delaney. She came up to them and smiled, her teeth a flash of white.

"Hey, Kala," Xander said.

"It's been a while," Kala replied. "I was afraid I'd lost one of my best customers."

"Course not. Just didn't make it by last time I was in town."

"Who's the boy?" she asked, looking down at Jacob.

103

"His name's Jacob," he replied. "It's a long story."

"My favorite kind," she said. "Hello, Jacob."

"Are those real?" Jacob asked.

"He means your eyes," Xander added.

Kala laughed. "Yeah, they're real." She reached up with one hand and popped a gold concave disc from one eye revealing a hazel iris. "Fake lenses, that's all. Don't tell me you've never seen these before?"

"He doesn't get out much," Xander broke in. "So what do you got, Kala? Anything new?"

"A shipment came in last week," she said. She turned and headed for the back of the shop. Xander followed. "The usual stuff. I've got a few you might like."

"I'll be a few minutes," Xander called back. "Feel free to look around."

While Xander and the woman lingered over a crate in the back corner of the store, Jacob wandered the silent aisles. From time to time, he pulled a book off its shelf and paged through it. Like the books at Xander's house, some had hard covers, others had covers not much thicker than the pages themselves. Some looked brand-new, while others looked ancient. He especially liked the ones with pictures on the cover, each revealing strange new worlds, suggesting what wonders might be within. Despite his earlier wish to read the street signs, it suddenly didn't matter that he couldn't read these books. Just the thought that each one contained new ideas, people, and places was enough to provide him a sense of peace. It reminded him how isolated he'd been in Harmony, a place where new ideas—or any ideas at all besides those of Truesight—weren't allowed or even acknowledged.

The strange thing was, he didn't completely disagree with his people's perception of the Seers. He'd seen enough of Melville to realize it was a world in which appearances dominated, and he'd certainly seen enough shallowness these last few weeks—from the teenagers at the lake to the abrasive veneer of LaPerle's grin—to more than justify the Blinders' scorn. But that was why he loved the quiet of this store, of being here right now. These books showed him that there was more to the Seers than what he'd encountered so far. There were elements of a full life ready for the taking if one wanted to find them. At least the Seers had a chance to do whatever they wanted with their lives.

"Ready?" Xander asked.

Jacob turned to see Xander and Kala watching him.

"Sorry. I was thinking about something," Jacob said.

"That tends to happen when people come in here," Kala said. "Here," she said, handing him a book.

Jacob took it. "For me? I don't have any money."

"It's a gift," she said.

"I don't know how to read," Jacob admitted.

She nodded. "That's okay—you can use it to learn. Besides, it's got pictures, as well."

He opened the cover and flipped through the pages. Each one contained a single image that was a blend of color, words, and pictures. The letters were thin and arched, scrawling across the page in a single stream. The pictures themselves were haunting. Like the words, they too flowed, tinged with colors of the moons and grass, the brilliant hues of flowers. In some ways, the busy pages reminded him of Melville, but at the same time they lacked the polish and angular edges of the city. They had an organic feel that went against the urban grain.

"What is this book?" he asked.

"It's by William Blake," Kala said. "He's a writer from Earth. From a long time ago. The book is called *Songs of Innocence and Experience*. Each page is a poem. You know, like a song made up of words? He wrote the poems and drew all those pictures."

Coming across one page, he was met by a familiar scene.

"Sheep," he said. "We have those where I come from."

"That one's called 'The Lamb,'" she said, glancing down at the page. "I'm sure Xander can read it to you later."

Xander frowned. "I'm not a big one for nursery rhymes," he said. "But thanks for the book, Kala. And these too." He held up the package in his hands.

"Any time," Kala replied.

Xander nodded to Jacob and headed for the door. Jacob waved good-bye to Kala and followed.

"See you in a few weeks," Kala called after them.

"Right," said Xander.

"I liked her," Jacob said as they left the store and headed down the alley back to the main avenue.

Xander nodded. "I've bought most of my books from her," he said. "Decent woman."

"Why was her skin that color? That strange purple?"

"Some people have different skin color. Just like they do hair. Though in Kala's case, it's intentional. There's a dye you can take—changes your skin to whatever color you want. For a while, anyway."

"What for?" Jacob asked.

"Something different, I guess," Xander said, shrugging. "Because she can. I don't know, I never asked. People do all kinds of things to make themselves look different."

They reached the avenue and continued on their way. Jacob was still thinking about the bookstore when the sight of Delaney froze him in his tracks.

She rose above him, above all of them on the street, appearing from nowhere against the side of a nearby tower. She had gone from the six-inch figurine in the palm of LaPerle's hand to a sixty-foot tall giant looking down with her gold-rimmed eyes. Letters flashed around her, words scrolling by as she smiled and an invisible wind lifted her hair. There was blue sky behind her with clouds racing by as if time had speeded up. But Delaney wasn't speeding—she moved slowly, her body swaying to a nonexistent song as time took her in the opposite direction. Jacob blinked at the image. He had seen Delaney once, enough to recognize her along the building's surface, but the weaving figure seemed like a stranger.

"You see her?" he asked, wondering if she was just a dream.

"Yeah, I see her," Xander replied.

"What do those words say?" Jacob asked.

"They're selling her," Xander said. "Or a version of her, anyway. Come on, let's get out of here."

He pulled Jacob over to a kiosk on the corner and pressed a circle displayed on its blue screen. A moment later, a floater pulled over to the curb beside them. They climbed into the backseat and the craft began rising.

"Where to?" asked the driver over his shoulder.

"Anywhere," Xander replied. "We just want out of Melville for a while."

"How about the sea?" Jacob asked, remembering what Delaney had told him.

"Sure," the driver said. They were now a couple hundred feet off the ground. All the way up, Jacob's stomach fluttered as the craft buoyed lightly up and down on its gravity pad. Now he had the sensation that he'd left his stomach behind as the floater leapt forward, zipping toward a tower face before cutting sharply between another set of buildings.

Jacob closed his eyes and leaned into Xander. The cruiser, speeding and bouncing along the plains, had been bad enough, but at least it was connected to the earth. This was far worse. He was sure that any minute the slim floater would overturn or tip too far on a corner and send them hurling toward the surface.

"Don't like flying?" Xander shouted in his ear above the wind roaring through the open cockpit.

"No!" Jacob screamed back. In fact, he hated everything about the sensation, especially the howling in his ears that made thinking impossible. Xander shouted something to the driver that he couldn't make out. A moment later, the roaring stopped as the compartment went silent.

"Go ahead, open your eyes," Xander told him.

Jacob opened his eyes and looked around. The city was gone. He glanced over his shoulder and saw the towers shrinking behind him. He looked up. The sky was still there, the sun still sinking toward afternoon. Where had the wind gone? He reached up and his hand met a solid but invisible plane.

"Force field," Xander explained. "There's your ocean."

He pointed over the side and Jacob gazed down and drew a sharp breath. Delaney had been right. The waters reaching toward the western horizon were beautiful, an azure tone that made the green of the land more brilliant, particularly the archipelagoes of shining emeralds spreading out from the coast as if they'd been tossed or spilled across the surface of the sea by some giant hand.

"Do people live there?" Jacob asked, pointing to the islands.

"Some do, I suppose. Not many people live outside Melville."

"I'd like to live on an island someday," Jacob said.

"Suppose that makes sense. After all, you grew up on one."

Jacob blushed. It was true. Harmony was an island, cut off from the world in so many ways. But that wasn't the kind of island where he wanted to live. He wanted a place that was away from the world but not disconnected from it, where people could leave if they pleased, but chose to stay, a place where he belonged.

The driver reached up and touched part of the dash panel. Music filled the cabin. His fear subsiding, Jacob relaxed back into his seat and watched the sea. The song ended and another began. The sound of the piano now playing soothed him. For a moment, he felt like he was back in Harmony. Between his mother's, Delaney's, and his own playing he had listened to music every day; it had simply been a part of life's background. Hearing it now made him miss that. Maybe tonight's concert wouldn't be so bad after all.

A girl's voice came in over the piano, accompanied by drums and a host of other instruments. He sat up and leaned forward. It was Delaney. He recognized her voice immediately, in spite of the synthesized filter that altered it, giving it an otherworldly edge. His initial excitement faded as the song progressed. Musicians in Harmony as a whole frowned on synthesized music. When it was used, it was used sparingly and never on voices. Listening to the song, Jacob couldn't help but feel that the effects and accompanying drumbeats cheapened the purity of her voice. It was just like the image he'd seen displayed on the side of the building—a stranger packaged for public amusement, as artificial as her eyes.

"Can you turn it off?" Jacob asked the driver.

"Don't like this song?" the man asked, killing the sound. "My daughter loves it. Won't stop listening to the damn thing. Keeps going on about this new girl. I'm no expert, but far as I can tell, she's not much different from the rest of them. Another six months, nobody'll even remember her. Pretty girl, though. They say she used to be a Blinder. Hard to believe, isn't it?"

Jacob sank back into the seat and closed his eyes.

"I suppose it is," he whispered.

CHAPTER ELEVEN

By the time they reached the Marlboro later that evening, a crowd had already gathered, spilling out the doors and into the street. Jacob and Xander got in line and waited. Around them, people laughed and joked, made small talk, and even gossiped about Delaney.

"They say her eyes were designed by Charles Kivan himself," one woman said.

"I heard that they can see through walls," her friend replied.

"I had dinner with her last week," a man in front of Jacob boasted to his party.

"You did not!" someone challenged.

"I did. My brother-in-law's the assistant to the VP for marketing. He invited me."

"What was she like?" several asked.

"Boring, I thought," the man sniffed. "Didn't say much."

"She probably doesn't have a lot to say," a woman said. "You know what these starlets are like—they're all bubbleheads anyway."

"Give her a break," another woman countered. "She used to be a Blinder. You can't expect her to fit in."

Listening to them carry on about someone he'd spent a

part of almost every day with for the last three years, Jacob didn't know whether to be amused or aghast. Mostly, he felt sad. The things they were saying didn't describe the girl he knew, but he couldn't be sure he knew who she was now any more than they did.

The sound of a man sneezing broke Jacob from his thought. He glanced over his shoulder to see the man standing directly behind him cover his mouth and begin coughing. The woman with him patted him on the back.

"I told you to see the doctor this afternoon," she scolded.

"Just a touch of the flu," he replied, sneezing. "I'll be fine."

The man coughed again. The sound reminded Jacob of his former neighbor Tobin Fletcher. Shuddering, he remembered the dream he'd had soon after joining Xander, remembered the sight of Tobin being carried by on the stretcher, his eyes open in death, and later, his wife crying on the doorstep. In real life, back in Harmony, both Tobin and his wife had been sick. He wondered how they were doing now. The sense of déjà vu came upon him again and he thought of Delaney, how she had looked just like the person in his dreams. He had always thought dreams were just an echo of what a person loved or feared, an improvisation on the present or past. Now he couldn't help but wonder if they had any bearing on the future.

The line moved at a steady pace and before long they were at the doors. Xander handed a ticket to Jacob, who watched as each person stepped up to the scanner and placed their card into the slot. Each time, the tiny image of Delaney popped up, greeted the ticket holder, and thanked them. Soon it was Jacob's turn.

112

"Thank you," Delaney chirped. "Enjoy the show!"

I'll try, he thought, retrieving his ticket. Xander followed and the two went inside, with Delaney's voice repeating into the distance. *Thank you. Thank you. Thank you. Thank you . . .*

They entered a vast lobby and let the flow of people carry them up the curved staircase toward the hall. For a moment, the parade of concertgoers reminded him of the Gatherings back in Harmony, when everyone in the community filtered into the square for their regular sermon.

The comfort he had once felt in blindness, of being part of the group, of feeling the bodies around him, had since been replaced with unease. Now, amid the chattering, plodding crowd, he fought with the rousing urge to flee. He stared down at the patterned floor tiles and tried to push away the cacophony of voices. He tried to relax, to remember he was safe. *This gathering isn't for you*, he told himself. Reaching into his pocket and feeling the cool metal of the sounder, he remembered who the gathering was for. It didn't make him feel any better.

LaPerle had given them excellent seats. They sat down and waited. Neither spoke in the semidarkness of the vast hall. Every few moments a cool breeze washed over the crowd. It felt good to be out of the crush of people. Even the voices were subdued to a murmur now as people roamed in search of their seats. The only light in the chamber came from four spotlights shining out of each corner, converging on the center of the stage where a black grand piano rested on a glass platform.

They waited. Five minutes, ten. The lights faded and the hall went silent.

A gasp broke out from the audience as the hall filled with

light as beam after beam of color flashed through the air, intersecting, cutting, and twirling as the dome of the ceiling seemed to open to a blaze of infinite stars and swirling nebula. The beams widened, spread out into rainbow sheets that washed over the hall in waves, now punctured by a series of virtual fireworks that crashed and thundered over everyone.

As the fireworks subsided, a voice called out, "Ladies and gentlemen! A warm welcome for the Rim's hottest new star—the beautiful, the mysterious . . . Delaney!"

The crowd erupted in a wild cheer as a single beam flashed onto a spot on the floor below them. Jacob leaned sideways to see around the person in front of him. His eyes widened.

Delaney stood, her head down, arms at her side. Her black hair, gathered up in a series of braids, shone in the brilliant white light, matching the shimmer of her loose, almost transparent gown. She began rising through the air, raised from the floor to the stage on a nearly invisible platform of glass that made her seem to hover with a will of her own.

Reaching the level of the stage, she strode to the piano, the crowd still clapping. Jacob glanced up at Xander. He was applauding too, his eyes fixed on the glowing figure before them. Looking back to Delaney, Jacob found himself clapping as hard as any of them—it was impossible not to. She was so beautiful, so serene. And she hadn't even started to play.

She took her seat at the piano and the crowd quieted. Softly, she began. The notes rippled over the audience. There was the slightest noise in response, as if the entire crowd joined in a collective sigh. Even Jacob was taken aback by the richness of the instrument. It made the piano he'd grown up with sound like a plinky child's toy, like the music box he'd listened to growing up.

Jacob suddenly realized she was playing the song he'd heard on the radio back in the floater. Sure enough, a moment later the piano was joined by the full blast of invisible synthesizers and drum machines as she began singing. *At least they left her voice alone*, he thought as he listened to it, amplified but unprocessed.

For the second time that evening, the crowd broke into a sudden, single gasp. The lights faded to a rosy hue. But the audience wasn't responding to the change of lighting, it was reacting to the vast image of Delaney hovering over the hall, occupying the darkness above the stage.

Jacob sank back and gripped the arms of his seat at the sight of the three-dimensional image above him. Glancing down at the stage, he realized the projection was in sync with the real girl below, but the floating form was just a disembodied head. The angle of the projection was head-on, slightly elevated, as if it was the audience who was in fact hovering before her. Every part of her face was magnified—every hair along her eyebrows, every freckle across her nose and cheeks, the sheen on her lips that glistened while she sang. But it was the eyes that dominated her face, that occupied the center of the angled view, those jeweled eyes that didn't move, that showed no emotion but simply glowed. Jacob grit his teeth and looked away.

"It's okay, Jacob," Xander said in his ear. "It's just a hologram. It isn't real."

Jacob didn't respond. Yes, he knew the head was a projection. But it was real, as real as it had been in the early hours of this morning as he lay in bed dreaming. Once again,

115

an image of his nightmare was playing itself out before his eyes.

The song ended and the crowd exploded in applause. Delaney thanked them, but Jacob barely heard. He just kept his eyes closed and hoped the show would be over soon. She started a new song. Listening in spite of himself, he wondered who wrote the songs. Clearly they weren't hers. This one was a love song of some kind, something about a girl who misses her boy. He's been out to space and won't be coming home for a long time, and she doesn't know what she's going to do, do, do . . .

Jacob opened his eyes. She was still there above him, but he found that if he kept his focus on the stage, he could pretend the head wasn't there. As the song continued, he started looking around at the crowd. They all stared with rapture on their faces, but their eyes weren't trained on Delaney. They were fixed upon the projection hanging in space, inflated and insubstantial.

The song ended. She began another, and then another. But as she continued, Jacob noticed something. At first he wasn't sure. It started with a single sour note. He cocked his head and focused. Soon came another. She had misplayed. Now her timing started to slip. She came in late on a chorus, missed the pickup after the bridge. A flash caught his eye, and he looked up at the hologram. Sure enough, her eyes had begun to sparkle. They were few and far between, but now and then he caught a flicker that flared across the surface of her eyes.

Not many seemed to notice her mistakes, though there were whispers in the hall as the last song ended. There was a long pause. The crowd silenced again.

116

"Is she all right?" Xander whispered.

"Something's wrong," Jacob said. He wanted to call out to her, let her know he was there. He wanted to rush up on stage and take her away, do something to help her.

She began playing again. This time there was no accompaniment, not even her voice. This time Jacob knew the song. It was his song, the one she'd written for him alone, a waltz, lulling and pure.

The crowd grew still. The piece was simple and unadorned, so different from anything she'd played so far. Listening to the song unfold, Jacob wondered if she'd planned ahead of time to play it. Did she know he was in the crowd? Was she playing this for him or for herself? He supposed it didn't matter.

His eyelids had begun to lower when once again, her fingers slipped. His eyes snapped back open. A moment later, another misplayed chord made him wince. She slowed down, then stopped altogether. An exchange of whispers, loud and hissing, ran around the hall. She started back in, picking up where she left off.

She only got a few measures. Another slip, then another, and once again she halted. The noise of the crowd now grew from a whisper to a murmur, and though the words were indistinguishable, the tone was not. A blend of curiosity and dismay with the slightest hint of amusement, it was derisive and cold. The hologram hanging above them faded quickly and the lights rose back to white. Suddenly, Delaney seemed more isolated than before. Before she'd been the hub, holding all of them in. Now she was the center of a crater from which they'd drawn back in confusion.

Delaney looked from the keyboard, first out at the crowd

117

and then up, tilting her head as if she were watching a butterfly flit above her or a high-soaring bird. The crowd grew quiet once again, waiting for her to make the next move. It didn't take long. Looking down, she stretched out her hands, spreading her fingers over the keys as if she was ready to resume the performance so they could all pretend the interruption had never taken place. Jacob could sense it in the crowd. She had only to start a new song and all would be forgotten.

Blam!

Her hands smashed down on the keyboard, creating a single dissonance that shattered the silence and jolted the crowd, pushing the audience back against their seats in stunned unison.

Delaney stood, shoved back the piano bench, and made a beeline for the edge of the elevated stage. The crowd gasped as she approached, striding across the glass platform with determined steps, seeming to walk on air. Jacob leaned forward, fighting the urge to leap up and make for the pit below. Stopping short at the edge, she stamped once against the glass and the section underfoot descended, carrying her to the floor.

The audience was on its feet now and the silence was shattered by a collective buzz of confusion. By the time Jacob managed to catch a glimpse down below, Delaney had disappeared. The house lights came on.

"Let's go," Xander shouted to him.

He brushed by Jacob and—to Jacob's confusion—headed down toward the stage. Though the crowd had begun to mill about, the two of them had aisle seats and it didn't take long to push through to the railing that circled the edge.

"What are you doing?" Jacob said as Xander climbed over the railing and dropped into the pit below.

"Come on. Hurry up!" Xander shouted, lifting his arms and beckoning with his hands.

A few people had come to the edge and were looking down at him, pointing. Jacob glanced around, expecting to see a group of men coming to grab him up, but all he saw was a few curious spectators and a sea of oblivious concertgoers jabbering about what had just transpired. He looked back down to where Xander waited. From here, it looked like a long drop.

"It's too high!" Jacob shouted.

"I'll catch you," Xander called back. "Trust me. Now let's go!"

Shaking his head, Jacob clambered over the railing and lowered himself until he was sitting on the edge about four feet above Xander. Closing his eyes, he pushed off. There was a second of falling before Xander caught him and lowered him to the ground.

"This way," Xander said and headed for the door from which Delaney had first appeared. Jacob followed.

The door led to a dark corridor that ran about a hundred feet before joining another. This second hallway was wider, with a series of doors along both sides. Xander immediately began making his way down the hall, opening one door after another, each revealing an empty dressing room. On the fifth try, they found her.

Like the first time they'd visited her, her back was to them. She sat before a mirror at a dressing table. Her head was down, buried in her arms, but she was quiet, not crying as Jacob first thought. They came in and closed the door.

"Don't say anything," she snapped. "I don't want you to say anything. I don't care about the stupid show."

"Are you all right, Delaney?" Jacob said.

Her head shot up. Jacob could see her face reflected in the mirror. She broke into a smile and turned.

"Jacob!" she cried. She rose and came over, embracing him. "I'm so glad you're here. I've been waiting for you to come back. I told Jack to expect you."

"Jack hasn't exactly been accommodating," Xander said.

Delaney frowned. "What do you mean?"

Jacob broke in. "Delaney, what happened out there on stage?"

She sighed and turned away. Returning to her seat, she leaned in toward the mirror and traced the gold along the edges of her eyes with her fingers before burying her face in her hands again.

"It's these eyes," she said at last. "They've ruined my music. I can't concentrate—I start watching my fingers as I'm playing and it gets me confused and then . . ." She drifted into silence.

Jacob came over and put his hands on her shoulders. She picked up her head again. He gazed down at her reflection in the mirror, uncertain if she was looking at him or at herself.

"I hate them," she blurted out. "I never thought I'd say it, but it's true. They're too much, Jacob. It's all too much." She shook her head.

"You said you liked seeing," he said.

"I did at first," she replied, "but it's exhausting. They're always on! I can't turn them off. I try to cover them up, but the light never goes away. You don't know what it's like. Nights are the worst. I haven't had a real night's sleep since the surgery."

She turned and pulled him down to her.

"Not only that, I think I'm losing them." She was whispering now, looking around as if someone else were present in the room. "They're not working right. These last few days, I have moments of static. Everything goes white, like I'm blind all over again. And after it fades, nothing looks the same. The colors are duller, the lights are dimmer. It's like everything is fading away. I feel like *I'm* fading away."

"But I thought you were happy."

"I was!" she declared. "Or at least, I think I was. I don't even know anymore. And then when you came . . . I wanted you to think I knew what I was doing, that I'd done the right thing. I wanted to make myself think that." She groaned. "Oh, Jacob, after everything that happened in Harmony, all the things I said . . ." Her voice rose, took on an edge that made Jacob's stomach sink. He'd heard that voice before, that tone of desperation those last days in Harmony. She gripped his hands so hard he winced. "What's wrong with me, Jacob?"

Before Jacob could respond, the door opened.

"What the hell was that out there?" LaPerle barked as he stormed into the room, followed by Karl. Seeing Jacob and Xander, he pulled up short and glared.

"I should have known," he said. He went over to Delaney and, brushing Jacob aside, placed his hands on her shoulder. "Poor, sweet Delaney. What happened out there?"

He didn't wait for her to answer. "Never mind about that. Everyone has a bad moment early on. You've just had yours. Good. Now it's out of the way and you can move on. I mean, it's a bit of a setback—the performance was being broadcast all over the Rim—but we'll work with it. Who knows? Maybe we can play it to our advantage—add a little mystery to your image. And there's always the sympathy vote."

He spoke quickly, his voice taking on a forced edge of cheer that couldn't quite mask his annoyance. For her part, Delaney said nothing, but Jacob could see her shoulders sag, the corners of her mouth turn down as LaPerle rambled. Suddenly, the man turned to Jacob.

"So nice of you to come by," he said. "I'm sure seeing you helped lift Delaney's spirits. Karl can show you the way out— this place is quite a maze."

"But we just got here!" Jacob exclaimed.

"Can't they stay?" Delaney said. "I want Jacob to stay with me. He can sleep over in my suite tonight. There's plenty of room. Please, Jack."

LaPerle knelt down before Delaney so that his head was level with hers. "You know I'd do anything for you," he said. "I told you so when you first came aboard, remember? Now, listen to me. You've had a difficult night. A terrible night. The thing you need most is to get some sleep without any distractions."

"But, Jack . . ." she pleaded.

"Now listen, Delaney. I told your friends earlier that we could arrange a visit. Soon. We'll make it real soon. Okay?"

She said nothing, but gave a slight nod. LaPerle rose.

"Gentlemen?" he said, gesturing toward the door.

They started to file out. On his way by Delaney, Jacob stopped and leaned down and the two of them embraced. Xander and Karl went out into the hall, while LaPerle waited in the doorway.

"I'll see you soon," he said to her.

"Right," she replied, trying to smile.

He slipped the sounder out of his pocket and placed it in her palm. "I thought you might want this back," he whispered.

Her hand closed over it. This time, she smiled for real.

Jacob rose and left, followed by LaPerle, who closed the door after them.

"It seems our little meetings have become quite a habit," he snapped, turning to face them. "And now look what you've done. See how you've upset her."

Xander snorted. "You're trying to pin what happened tonight on us?" he demanded.

"She was fine before you two showed up. Everything was on track. And now . . . well, you saw her out there tonight. There's a lot at stake here."

"For you," Xander retorted.

"For *all* of us," LaPerle said. "If this pans out, she'll never have another worry the rest of her days."

"And that's what this is all about, right?" Xander said.

"Why not?" LaPerle said. He shook his head. "I can't believe I'm wasting my time with you two. Enough. Karl, escort them out. And this time, make sure they get the message."

He turned and went back into the dressing room, slamming the door behind him. Frowning, Karl passed them and headed down the hall. "Let's go," he snapped.

They followed him down a series of corridors toward the lobby.

"Karl," Xander said after a few minutes of walking. Karl ignored him. He just kept his body plowing forward. "Karl!" Xander barked.

Karl drew up so fast they nearly collided with him. "Just shut up, Xander," he growled, his back still to them. He continued. A few moments later they came to a door and Karl turned to face them. "You wouldn't listen to me before, so listen now. Stay away from the girl. Stay away from Mixel."

123

"You sound like one of them," Xander said.

"Christ, Xander," Karl said, shaking his head. "Why are you doing this to me?"

"I'd ask you the same question. What's this handler got about us coming around?"

"I don't ask questions, I just do what they tell me. You remember what that was like, don't you?"

"Why do you think I left?"

Karl snorted. "We both know why you left." He opened the door. Beyond it they could see the lobby. Xander walked out with Jacob in tow, then stopped and faced Karl who stood in the doorway.

"See you later, pal," Xander scoffed.

"Look, I remember everything we went through together," Karl said, "and I know you do too. But next time I see you, there'll be trouble. I'm not risking my job over this. It's just business. That's all."

"Just business," Xander said. "That was always our line, wasn't it?"

Karl nodded and closed the door.

The sky was dark as they left the concert hall. Night had come quickly. They made their way to the cruiser in silence.

"Why *doesn't* LaPerle want us near Delaney?" Jacob asked finally as they turned into the alley.

"Control," Xander replied. It was too dark for Jacob to see Xander's face, but Jacob could hear it in his voice: that bitterness, an edge darker than the sky above them. "It's nothing personal. Just business. They want her to depend only on them. If we're around, if you're in her life, it makes it harder for that to happen. They want to keep her isolated."

"I know what that's like," Jacob replied.

They got in the cruiser and drove away, leaving the lights of the city behind. Looking back, Jacob could almost see Delaney's face still hovering, opaque above the towers, her eyes absorbing the city's glow, unable to tear themselves away.

CHAPTER TWELVE

Jacob woke up the next morning angry. He wasn't sure at first what had seeded his anger or when. He'd slept most of the return trip, dozing on and off, losing himself in the vibration of the cruiser. The entire drive back he was numb. After the long day in Melville, he had nothing left. All that remained was a hollow space inside him—everything vital had been drained by disappointment. Arriving back at the house, he'd stumbled to bed with hardly a word.

That evening the customary nightmare was gone, replaced by an entirely new one—he was no longer pacing the streets of his old home. The scene had shifted to Melville. He looked into the sky. The moon was bright and large. He looked again: it was pink and cratered; it was Drake, not Druna. Why was it so close? *It's going to hit us. We're going to collide.* He looked even closer. There were people on the moon, little dark shapes crawling like insects, kicking up puffs of pink moon powder. Someone tapped him on the shoulder, and without looking back he ran. Now he was the one being chased. He didn't try to see who it was. He didn't need to. He could hear her voice behind him, as if she were leaning forward, whispering in his ear.

"I knew you would," she said.

Over and over her words repeated as he ran an endless loop around the streets. A story that went nowhere, it was far worse than the usual nightmare, and he awoke in a dark mood.

The dream faded but his anger didn't as he remembered LaPerle in the dressing room last night, remembered Delaney sitting quiet and dejected while Jacob had walked out and left her yet again. Jacob was mad at the man, but more so at himself. He hadn't been there for Delaney back in Harmony when she floundered, and he'd sworn that, given the chance, he wouldn't let it happen again, wouldn't leave her to her misery. But here he was, making the same mistake all over again.

"We have to go get her," he told Xander at breakfast.

"Don't worry. You'll meet up with her again. After last night, I don't see her going to Earth any time soon."

"I mean we have to get her out of there. We have to bring her back here."

There was a long pause. Xander looked down at his breakfast.

"No," he said at last.

"What?" Jacob cried, jumping up from the table. It had never occurred to him that Xander would refuse. The man had been so determined about helping Jacob visit Delaney, had such clear disdain for her handler, he couldn't imagine why he'd hold back now.

"You heard me."

"But you were *there* yesterday!" Jacob exclaimed. "You heard what she said. We have to save her."

"Save her, huh? The princess in the tower?" Xander got up and went to the window. "Look, Blinder, I don't mind bringing you into Melville to see your friend, but I draw the line at kidnapping."

"It's not kidnapping if she wants to come."

"You don't know what she wants. Neither does she. She was upset when you saw her. It was a bad moment. For all we know, she might have woken up this morning and realized things were pretty good after all."

"You don't believe that. You even said before that she seemed miserable."

"Forget what I said," Xander snapped.

"But you hate that man LaPerle, you said as much to Karl. Do you want him to win?"

"Win what? It's not a game, Jacob. LaPerle's nothing to me."

"I guess Delaney's nothing to you, too."

"Well, she is *your* friend."

"Is this because of Karl? Or are you afraid?" Before Jacob could stop himself, he had blurted it out. Plopping down in his chair, he glanced nervously at Xander. There was a long silence.

"I left fear behind years ago," the man finally replied, looking out the window. His voice was icy and his fingers gripping the wood of the windowpane were white. "I just don't feel like having another Blinder around to take care of. One is bad enough." He spun and glared down at Jacob. "I didn't come out here to start a foster home. I came out to be alone. I came out here for some goddamn peace and quiet."

He turned and walked out of the house, leaving the door open behind him. Jacob didn't have to follow him to know where he was going. Sure enough, a moment later there was the growl of the cruiser's engine firing up. He listened as its roar faded into the distance.

Jacob stood up from the table and walked out onto the deck. Reaching for the railing, he could see his hands trembling. *Did that just happen?* he wondered. His recent nightmares seemed more real than this moment. The last few weeks, he'd gotten used to the man, had gotten used to this place. He hadn't thought Xander would turn on him. He had been fooled into thinking Xander didn't mind having him around, that maybe he even liked his company. And now he had pushed too far, had drawn the truth from his host. He wasn't wanted here. A sickness rose in him. This man was his only connection to the world. Where would Jacob go if Xander cut him off? How would he survive? The image of the skeleton in the grass flashed into his mind. Somewhere to the east, in the basin of a valley, the lonely bones still lay.

No, Jacob thought. *He would have asked me to leave if he'd wanted me gone. He didn't mean what he said. He's just angry, like he always gets.*

He relaxed his grip on the railing and looked out. The day was hot. The sun shone, but the sky had faded from blue to gray as a thin layer of clouds had crept in overnight, turning the sun silver. Squinting, he could just make out the black sliver of Mixel Tower through the haze. Delaney was in that tower. Maybe she was looking through her window right now, looking straight at him without even knowing it, hoping for a way out. Before he'd been to Melville, before he'd seen the world of the Seers, he thought he could find her and they'd live happily ever after. Now he knew better. Even if he could sneak in to see her, LaPerle would never let him stay, and he couldn't get her out on his own. He needed Xander to help him.

He went inside and collapsed into one of the armchairs. There had to be some way of getting Xander to change his mind.

All morning and into the afternoon he lingered in the house, trying to devise a plan. Like Delaney, Xander was stubborn. And right now, he was angry. The first thing Jacob needed to do was get back into his good graces. Then maybe he could convince Xander to help him.

Jacob suddenly realized that he'd done virtually nothing to help out since he'd gotten here. Not that he'd been asked—Xander led a spartan life, regimented and independent. Still, even in Harmony he'd had chores to do at home, whether it was washing dishes or sweeping the floor of their underground house.

He cleaned up from breakfast as well as his own lunch and then started looking around for something else to do. At first he thought about cleaning the house, but it wasn't that dirty. Even so, he could at least sweep the floor.

Looking for a broom, he tried a door that was tucked around a corner under the staircase. He'd noticed it before and assumed it was a closet. He instead found a set of stairs leading down into the darkness of a basement. His thoughts of sweeping forgotten, he turned on the light and headed down the steps.

The basement was cool and spare, even more so than the floors above. The concrete walls and earthy smell reminded him of the underground buildings in Harmony, and when he closed his eyes for a second, he could have sworn he was home. There were a few metal cylinders lined up in the corner. On the face of one was a tiny, lit screen, and all of them had several lights and dials along the front, as well as wires and tubes running from them up into the ceiling. The machines reminded Jacob of the ghostbox. He shivered and looked away to the other side of the room. A pile of boxes lay stacked against the wall, neatly ordered, aside from one crate that sat alone, separated from its companions. It looked like all the others, but just gazing at it, Jacob felt a chill run down his back. It was that same prickling sensation he'd felt the day he'd found the body in the grass. He reached down to touch it. In the back of his mind, a tiny voice told him to stop, that he wasn't meant to open this box. *You shouldn't even be down here*, it said. But before he could listen, he'd popped open the clasp and lifted the cover.

He leaped back at the sight of the yellow creature with black beady eyes that looked up at him from the crate, and then he scrambled for the foot of the stairs. Only when he paused on the third step and looked back did he realize he'd left the cover open. For several seconds he waited, expecting the furry monster to leap out and give chase, but everything was still. Heart pounding, he slunk back toward the crate and popped his head up for a quick glance. The creature hadn't moved.

Approaching tentatively, Jacob closed in on the box and inspected it once more. The creature had remained frozen, and as Jacob leaned in, he realized there was something different about it, something about the eyes—a kind of deadness. Reaching down, he felt the body and laughed with relief.

Jacob stroked the animal's synthetic fur and gazed into its plastic eyes. He turned it over and noticed its hindquarters were dirty and the fibers along one back leg were singed. Overall, the animal had a burned scent, the smell of a fire that had died long ago.

Putting the creature aside, he returned to the crate. He had expected to find something different inside. Maybe weapons, like the ones he'd already seen Xander carry, or armor, something to do with war. Instead, there were other toys inside—balls, a few other stuffed animals, toy ships and cars, small soldiers dressed in strange-looking armor—as well as clothes, none of which looked big enough to fit him. Like the first creature he'd found, the items had the same smoky odor, not nearly as pleasant as the smell of burning zephyr wood.

Rummaging through the box, he was delighted to find an instrument. No, there were two: a whistle with six finger holes and some kind of harp. He pulled the whistle out and examined it. The whistle was made of burnished wood with a marbled texture that looked like swirling water. As for the harp, it was a child's toy. Still, plying his fingers across the strings, he discovered it had a decent sound. All it needed was a little tuning. He returned the harp to the crate and went back to examining the whistle.

His fingers fitted instinctively to the holes. He'd spent so many hours holding an instrument just like this growing up. Every child in Harmony learned to play the whistle. It was one of the initial classes they took in school. He remembered playing in his first concert—five years old, twenty-seven of them packed together, puffing out the tune of some nursery rhyme, a cacophony of song that brought laughter from parents and children alike. He'd loved the sound of his whistle and had practiced every afternoon in his room before supper for the next several years, even accompanying his mother while she played the songs she'd taught him on the piano.

Putting the instrument to his lips, Jacob blew a tentative

note. At first, he recoiled from the burnt taste, but the sound drew him back. He blew another note, held it, and listened to the breathy, whispered tone so pure he wished he could hold it forever. Even as his air ran out, its quavering had a sweetness.

An idea struck him. If there was one thing Jacob could do, it was play music. He could perform for his host, put on a concert of his own. Tonight he would surprise him with the gift.

But first he had to practice. It had been a few years since he'd played the whistle with any seriousness.

He started in, first with scales, running up and down the different sets with increasing speed until he could feel the quickness in his fingers once again. Then he advanced to some simple songs, beginning with the first he'd ever learned and moving on from there. Skipping from one tune to the next, it was as if he were growing up all over again. With each song came flashes of memory—the sound of a classmate's laugh, the scent of a certain flower or food, the pang of a particular joy or fear. He lost himself in the progression. At one point he realized he'd closed his eyes, but when he opened them, he discovered he couldn't play without them closed—it just didn't feel right.

Before long he'd run through the series of his childhood songs. They were nice, but he wanted something more, something that would really impress Xander. He started in on a sequence of melodies his mother had taught him during the last year before he'd abandoned the whistle for the piano and guitar. They were fairly intricate, inspired by classical pieces from ancient Earth, melodies of Bach, but imprinted with the modern sensibility of Harmony's own musicians. It took him several tries, but before long he had a number of them down and now began running through them over and over.

With his eyes closed, the trilling notes of the familiar songs combined with the earthy scent of the basement in a wave that carried him away. He was no longer Jacob, the boy who could see. He had never left the dark comfort of his home, had never been terrified by strange dreams that spilled over into his waking life, had never been the subject of violence or scorn. Before long, he could hear the sounds of his mother's piano. She was right beside him, her fingers flying with a speed to match his own, her notes cascading out and wrapping around his own tune, merging into a single song. He could hear her breathing, uttering the little sounds that often escaped her mouth as she played, unconscious accents to her music. A longing filled him. He had never missed anyone so much as he missed her now. And now she was talking, calling out the chord changes, calling out words of praise as he kept up with her ever-increasing tempo. She was calling to him once more.

"What the hell are you doing?"

The shouting jolted him from his song. For a brief second he felt that he was falling, before he snapped his eyes open and turned.

Xander was at the bottom of the steps. A darkness had fallen over the man's face, making him look more fearsome than ever. He came toward Jacob with giant strides, though it seemed as if he were moving in slow motion. Jacob tried to move, tried to say something to ward off the man's advance, but he was frozen in place, the whistle still gripped between his fingers, suspended in air before him.

Jacob braced himself as Xander loomed over him. The man snatched the whistle from his hands, threw it back into the box, and slammed the lid so hard Jacob jumped. Without looking at Jacob, he turned and stormed back up the stairs, slamming the basement door behind him.

For a long time, Jacob remained in the basement, trying to stop shaking. Sitting on the crate, he kept seeing the fury on the man's face. Again that stunned, surreal aura swept over him. He was sure he'd discovered a way of doing something nice for Xander, but now things were worse than ever. He felt he should go up and apologize, but who knew what kind of state Xander might still be in.

There was no sound of footsteps on the floor above since the thunder of Xander's boots leaving for the second time that day. So, after Jacob's heart had returned to normal, he crept back up the stairs and opened the door a crack. He saw no sign of Xander and came out into the main room. Going to the window, his heart surged at the sight of Xander's cruiser sitting in the yard. He hadn't left. He had to be close by. Jacob slipped out onto the deck, and looked around but saw no one.

He decided not to look any further and went back inside. Pacing the room, he tried to think of the words to say to Xander when he returned, fighting off the urge to just gather his few possessions, head for Melville, and take his chances there.

The afternoon hurried away, dusk crept in the windows, and still Xander didn't come back. Going out onto the deck, Jacob paused in the twilight at the familiar scent of burning zephyr wood and saw the glint of Xander's fire through the trees. *Go now*, a voice told him. *Go talk to him.*

He headed down the stairs, and crossing the yard, entered the path through the trees. His legs felt numb, and he took slow steps toward the fire, steps that became slower the closer he got. But at last he reached the clearing, came into the circle of the fire and sat down at his usual spot, silent. Xander never raised his eyes from the flames. It was as if Jacob were invisible, coming upon this man for the first time, unnoticed. It reminded him of his last days in Harmony when he had moved unseen among the people, watching them go about their lives, his neighbors never knowing he was at hand.

One minute passed into the next, piling up, weighting down the silence until Xander's voice broke the stillness.

"It was my last campaign," he said. "Fighting had broken out in a Mixel system. We'd been stationed there for a couple years—most of us had families there. My wife, my two boys— Mixel had set us up in some nice quarters. We'd fought some skirmishes in different parts of the sector, but business was slow and we all had lots of time at home. We were uneasy about the fighting once it got close, of course, but nearly all of it had been confined to orbit; things were peaceful on the ground."

He paused. Jacob could feel him struggle to continue.

"My platoon was topside, packed in shuttles on our way to raid a freighter, when we heard the news. By the time we got back, our settlement had disappeared. Barracks, residentials, everything bombed. Where our families had been was nothing but a pile of rubble."

Jacob gasped. It was as if, for the slightest moment, he could see the wreckage—the broken stone, the twisted metal. Then the image faded, leaving him with nothing but the memory of the singed bear in the basement and the odor of acrid smoke that lingered over all the toys, just the faintest echo of destruction.

136

"I'm sorry," Jacob whispered. He didn't know what else to say. But now he knew what Karl's cryptic words of consolation had meant, not to mention Xander's stormy reaction that first night at the fire when he'd asked him about his family.

Xander snorted in disgust. "It was Mixel that did the bombing. They'd gotten word that the enemy had established a base on the surface and were determined to get rid of it. But it turned out to be a setup. The other corporation had sent a false report, disguised of course, and at the last minute hacked in and changed the bombing coordinates."

"They'd really do that?"

"Well, that was Mixel's story. Whatever really happened, Mixel screwed up—even if their story's true, they could've reconned the base to see if the report was accurate, or sent in a company for a ground assault, or had better ship security when they launched the attack, or a million other things. But they were in a rush and wanted a clean sweep."

"So what did you do?"

"What could I do? Mixel came to all of us who had lost our homes and families and offered us a deal—land rights in any Mixel colony, along with immediate retirement and full pensions if we didn't push for an investigation. They'd do anything to avoid the bad press and even more to prevent the trade sanctions that would follow. The writing was on the wall, so we took the deal. We'd all seen enough in our careers to know that when Mixel wants something, they get it, one way or another. That's why I'm here on Nova Campi. After all that, the only thing I wanted was to get away from the world, and this was the farthest I could go."

"And those things in the crate?"

"I spent two days picking through the wreckage. That was

about all I could find that was worth keeping."

"You didn't find them?"

"No, I found them," Xander murmured. He cleared his voice and for the first time looked up at Jacob. "Sorry if I scared you before," he said.

"I shouldn't have opened that box."

Xander shook his head. "It was just hard seeing you with that whistle. That was Marty's—my older boy. He'd be nearly your age now. I told my wife he was too young to learn to play an instrument, but she wouldn't listen. Said he'd grow into it."

"It's a nice whistle," Jacob offered.

"It sounded nice. You can keep it if you want. You play pretty well." He threw another log into the fire.

"I play okay, but not as good as Delaney. Almost every day when she'd come over for lessons, I'd just lie on the couch and listen to her and my mother play. Usually piano, sometimes harp or violin. It didn't matter. It was enough just to be around her."

Xander looked down at the dwindling flames. "You wouldn't think so, listening to you talk in your sleep."

"What do you mean?"

"You always sound terrified of her."

Jacob hesitated. A part of him didn't want to even think about his recurring dreams, let alone talk about them. But there was another part of him that did, that hoped that in the telling, the mysteries behind the dreams might be brought to light.

And so before he knew it, he began describing the dreams to Xander. He told him about being back in Harmony, about the habitual chase, the strange images and variations, and worst of all, the final confrontation at the end.

138

"Seeing those hands reaching out around her throat, the fire everywhere, it makes me sick. Why would I want to hurt her? Or her me? It doesn't make any sense."

"Dreams never do," Xander assured him.

"But these are so real—the fire in her eyes, the expanding head just like that projection at the concert, the fact that she looked the same in my dream before I ever saw her in real life. It's as if my dreams have come true. Not exactly, but close enough. Too close. It scares me."

"It's just a coincidence, Jacob. Reality and fantasy mix in nightmares. I know. I have them too."

Maybe Xander was right. After all, last night's dream had been different. It was still a nightmare, but there was no doubt in Jacob's mind that Delaney's accusatory voice chasing him through the streets of Melville was a product of his guilty conscience and his imagination working against him.

"Forget about your dreams," Xander said. "No point worrying about things you can't control."

"Maybe if we can be together, the nightmares will stop."

Xander didn't respond. Taking a stick, he stirred the collapsing remains of the fire, darkening the clearing.

Looking up through the opening in the trees, Jacob could see the outline of a ship passing low overhead, dragging a trail of light across the stars.

"What kind of ship is that?" Jacob asked, pointing at the sky.

"That's a trader's craft, a smaller one," Xander said. "Lots of them make their way to Nova Campi. Mixel has their own fleet of cargo liners, but they've got plenty of freelancers working on the side."

"What's it like?" Jacob asked.

"What, riding in a ship?"

"Being in space."

"It depends. It can be beautiful. It can be boring. And sometimes, it can make you feel lonelier than you'd ever thought you could feel."

"I remember the first time I saw a ship, the night before I ran away from Harmony. It looked so peaceful up there in the sky, so far away from anyone's problems. I just wished I could be on that ship. It didn't matter where it was going, I just wanted to be up there. "

"Maybe you will one day. Some people are drawn to space. They wouldn't want to be any place else."

"I wish I had a place like that, where I fit in, and things made sense."

"You and me both," Xander said.

He got up and headed for the house. Jacob watched him disappear and thought once more about the story Xander had told him. He took one last look at the fallen embers, their red glow already starting to fade, and then followed Xander from a distance.

They hardly spoke at dinner and went to bed soon after. It took Jacob a long time to doze off. He kept seeing Xander picking through a pile of smoldering rubble. Finally, he gave in to sleep, and then to his recurring nightmare. It had a new intensity. Never before had the tunnel seemed so dark, never before had the fire from Delaney's eyes burned so hot. As the fire overwhelmed him, Jacob awoke to find himself soaked in sweat, the sheets drenched. Taking the blanket folded at his feet, he slipped out of bed and curled up on the floor, wrapping the blanket around himself. For the remaining hours of

140

the night, the burning sensation lingered. He slept fitfully and was grateful when morning finally came.

Hearing Xander get up and go downstairs, Jacob rose and got dressed. He felt woozy at first, but by the time breakfast was ready he was better, last night just a memory.

Breakfast was as quiet as dinner had been, and Jacob had started to worry that Xander had fallen back into anger. All morning the man was withdrawn. When Jacob spoke to him, he acted as if he'd barely heard him, taking his time to respond and, even then, saying little. When he left the house after lunch, Jacob debated whether to follow, but Xander returned a few minutes later.

"We leave in five minutes. You'd better get ready," he said.

Jacob froze. "For what?"

"We're going to Melville."

He gave Jacob a smile, then turned and went back outside.

All the darkness Jacob had felt the last two days—the anger, the fear, the homesickness, the regret—all of it washed away in an instant. He grabbed his jacket, and was headed for the door, when he suddenly stopped. He was sure he knew where Delaney was, but he didn't want to take any chances. He turned and went up the stairs, down the hall, and into his room, where he slid open the top drawer of his bureau. The drawer was empty but for one item, the only thing of value he possessed. He grabbed the finder, put it in his pocket, and left.

CHAPTER THIRTEEN

"So what made you change your mind?" Jacob shouted over the throb of the cruiser as Melville's towers rose before them.

Xander shrugged. "Got tired of listening to you scream at night," he shouted back.

Jacob knew he was only half-serious but decided not to press the matter, afraid the man might change his mind. Besides, what difference did it really make? What mattered was that soon Delaney would be with them. Hopefully.

"How are we going to do this, anyway?" Jacob asked an hour later as they pulled over and parked the cruiser several blocks away from Mixel Tower. "LaPerle isn't going to let us take her."

"You're right. We can't just walk in as we are—they're ready for us now. We'll have to sneak in. And that's going to take some thought, not to mention some special toys."

"Like what?"

"You'll see."

Jacob started to get out. He paused to watch Xander open the dashboard compartment and retrieve a small pistol. After checking a few switches, the man slipped it into his shirt pocket.

"What?" he demanded, looking at Jacob's widening eyes.

"Nothing," Jacob said. "I just didn't think about having a gun."

"Relax. It's just a stunner. We may need it."

"Okay," he whispered.

Xander gave a brief smile. He got out of the cruiser and helped Jacob down onto the street. They went in the opposite direction of Mixel headquarters, toward the center of the city. As they walked, Jacob kept thinking about the gun in Xander's pocket and of Karl's warning the last time they met.

Soon, they were on the main avenue. It was noon, and the streets were packed with people heading out for lunch and midday shopping. Jacob still wasn't used to the sound of voices, music, and vehicles converging around him, or to the barrage of colors, lights, and movement. He found himself, as before, clinging tightly to Xander.

"When do we go back to Mixel?" Jacob asked.

"Tonight. We'll try to hit it at the end of the day. The lobby will be swarming with people headed home. That's when we'll have the best chance of blending in."

A few minutes later, they turned off the main avenue and onto a familiar narrow street. As before, the lamp marking Kala's bookstore glowed in the deep shadow of the buildings.

"We're going to get some books?" Jacob asked. "How does that help?"

"We're not going for books, Blinder. The things we need you can't buy in any store. Kala may sell books now, but she didn't use to. She knows the right people in Melville, the ones we need to see."

"What did she do before?" Jacob asked.

"Most everyone in Melville either works for Mixel or used to. We're all one big happy family," he quipped. "Kala's no exception. After Mixel she moved into, well, other areas. Once she'd made enough money, she decided to get out and spend her time with something she really loved."

"Books?"

"That's right."

The bell over the door rang as they entered. As before, the store was empty.

"Twice in three days. To what do I owe the honor?" Kala said, coming around the corner of a bookcase, her gold eyes flashing. "Or have you come to make a return?"

"Hey, Kala," Xander said. "Nothing like that."

"Then what can Kala do for you?" she said.

"We're looking for a few items. Hard-to-get items. You used to be in the business. Thought you might be able to help."

"*Used* to be in the business," she said. "I don't play those games anymore, Xander. You know that."

"I know, Kala. Just a name, a place, somebody we might go to."

She looked down at Jacob. "What's he getting you into?" she asked him.

"It was my idea," Jacob said, trying to hide the tremor in his voice.

"So *you're* the mastermind here," she said, smiling.

"Come on, Kala, go easy," Xander broke in. "It's nothing major. Not even illegal—at least, I don't think so. We just need to be someplace without anyone knowing we're there. That kind of thing."

"That kind of thing, huh?" she said. "All right, I'll help. You are my best customer after all. But you're going to need plenty of cash. He doesn't give the stuff away. Stay here."

144

She went to the back of the store. Jacob turned to Xander.

"What's cash?" Jacob whispered.

"Cash is money. You know, what you use to buy things with."

"But I don't have any money," Jacob hissed.

"I've got some," Xander replied.

"But she said we'd need a lot. I don't want you to use all of yours for me."

"Look, if we can't afford what I'd like to get, we'll just make do. It'll add to the challenge."

Kala returned and handed Xander a slip of paper. Xander opened it, read it, and laughed.

"Raker?" he said. "You got to be kidding me."

"Know him, huh? Figures. You were both mercs. Well, he's the man now."

Xander laughed again. "Thanks, Kala. I owe you," he said, slipping the paper into his pocket.

"Don't worry about it. Just don't get yourselves hurt, okay? Especially this one," she said, giving Jacob's shoulder a squeeze. "He's too cute."

Jacob's eyes widened at her words. Seeing the look on his face, she broke out laughing.

"Stop scaring the kid," Xander said. "Come on, Jacob. Let's go."

"Give Raker my best," Kala called out as they left the store.

Back on the main street, Xander broke into such a quick stride, Jacob practically had to trot to keep up.

"We might have struck a little bit of luck for once, if Raker's who I think he is," Xander said.

"Is he like Karl?"

145

"No. Karl's a buddy. Or was, anyway. Raker and I weren't that close. Didn't know each other long."

"So how is that good? Is he going to help us?"

Xander shrugged. "Maybe not. But I think he will. We worked together a few times early in my career. I saved his sorry butt the last time we went out. Carried him the better part of a mile out of the middle of a firefight. Don't even know why I did it—never really liked him. Not a bad guy, just kind of a baby. Anyway, looks like there was a reason for it after all."

"Let's hope," Jacob said.

They walked for about twenty minutes toward the edge of the city, putting downtown between themselves and Mixel Tower. From time to time, Jacob stole glances at the black structure dwarfing every other building in the city. Jacob wondered what they would find there, wondered what kind of shape Delaney would be in. What if Xander had been right yesterday? What if she didn't want to leave? All of this would be for nothing. Then another question came to mind.

"What if she isn't there?"

"Then we wait, I guess."

Glancing around, Jacob noticed that most of the stores and shopping centers had disappeared. In their place squatted enormous buildings that looked like much larger versions of the storage houses in Harmony: plain, boxlike, with few doors or windows. The crowd had likewise dwindled, trickling to an occasional passerby, and the floater and groundcar traffic had been replaced with large haulers scuttling between the buildings and a collection of concrete structures visible at the far end of the street. He guessed that the buildings were warehouses and factories of different kinds, but what were those strange bunkers ahead of them?

146

"We're heading toward the port," Xander said, as if anticipating Jacob's question.

No sooner had Xander spoken than the ground beneath Jacob's feet began to vibrate slightly, accompanied by a distant rumble that reminded him of the great storms that swept the plains from time to time. Jacob looked ahead in the direction of the noise and gasped. Not far away, a starship was lifting off from its bunker, rising above the concrete walls, drifting upward and rotating as it climbed. It was oblong, painted white with blue circles along its sides. He had a hard time figuring out how big it was. It didn't appear to be a huge ship from here, but he couldn't tell how far away it really was. They stopped walking and watched as it climbed into the sky like a feather riding a current of warm air before bursting forward with a flash of its engines. A moment later it had disappeared from sight.

Xander pointed ahead. "I think that's it."

They stopped at a corner. Across the street stood a steel warehouse, indistinguishable from all the others around it but for a set of numbers painted across the front. A single row of windows stretched the entire length of the building just below the roof several stories up. After waiting for a hauler to go by, they crossed the street and stood before the building.

"I don't see any door," Jacob said.

"Neither do I."

They walked down the street and around the corner to the other side. Still there was no door. They continued walking. Turning another corner they saw several large bays big enough for the haulers and, along the edge of the building, a side entrance. They went to the door and tried it. It was unlocked.

"We're in luck," Xander said.

"This is a weird place," Jacob said, looking around at the empty street. "Where is everybody?"

"Working, I guess. Let's go."

Coming in from the street, their eyes took a moment to adjust to the darkness. The windows along the top cast a dim light into the warehouse, enough to reveal its vast size but little else. Jacob was used to being inside dark spaces, but always tight, cozy ones like his house or his room, nothing this immense. It was like a huge cavern. To their left by the bay doors was a platform, but everything else around them was empty space, a black void. The floor underfoot was metal grating. It extended ten feet before them and ended in a staircase that descended into the dark.

The windows rattled as a nearby ship took off, its sound a muffled throb.

"I guess there's nowhere else to go but down," Xander said, his voice echoing in the dark. Though he stood right next to Jacob, he sounded far away. This place, this trip, it didn't feel right. Nothing felt right, Jacob realized. Over the last hour, he'd begun noticing the slightest feeling of wooziness coupled with a warmth gathering in his forehead, an echo of this morning that now simmered at the edges of his awareness.

They started down the stairs, their boots clanging against the metal steps, sounding all the louder against the hollow silence. The staircase turned back and forth, zigzagging every twenty steps.

"Back in the store with Kala, both of you kept saying 'the business.' What business were you talking about?" Jacob asked.

"Smuggling. Certain things are illegal, but people still want them. So other people like Raker provide them."

"Don't they get caught?"

"Now and then, I guess. But hardly ever, unless it's something really bad. The corporations that run these planets mostly turn a blind eye. Hell, some of them probably get a take of the action."

It reminded Jacob of all the bad things his people had told him about the Seers back in Harmony. But the people of Harmony also turned a *blind* eye to the corruption in their midst. The only difference was the Seers did it by choice. Which was worse?

A minute later, they reached the bottom of the stairs. The light from above was almost nonexistent here, barely enough to illuminate the cargo crates and containers rising above them, stacked into piles that loomed like buildings, creating narrow streets between them. Down at the end of one of these corridors, Jacob could see a light.

"Is that where we're supposed to go?" he asked Xander.

"We're about to find out," the man replied.

They started toward the light. As they got closer, a dull throb began to emerge. At first, Jacob thought it was the sound of his pulse—his heart was pounding harder with every step as a growing nervousness spread out from his stomach. But as they continued the sound grew louder and took on a rhythm different from his heart. For a moment, he thought it must be another ship taking off, but it wasn't the slow, steady roar he'd heard up on the street. It was too frenetic, rising and falling in a wave of sound.

It's music, Jacob realized as they approached.

Now he could make out the source of the light, could see

149

the blue lamp over a door. Then he stopped. A man was sitting beside the door.

"Come on, Blinder. Don't worry," Xander said, looking back.

As they walked up to the doorway, the man rose from his chair. Jacob edged closer to Xander and looked up at the man with wide eyes. In the glow of the lamp, the man's face was rough, the shadows exaggerating his craggy features. His hair was long and unkempt, not pulled back but hanging around his face like tendrils of prairie grass grown wild. He was shorter than Xander, but seemed bulkier, though it was hard to tell under his baggy clothes. As the muffled pulse of bass and drums shuddered behind the door, like a beast struggling to get out, he looked the two of them over.

"Haven't seen you before," he said.

"We're here for Raker," Xander replied.

"Of course you are," the man replied. "Everyone is. But not this time of day. It's early. And you've got a kid. What's the idea of that?"

"Can't be helped," Xander snapped. "I'll have him keep his eyes closed if it makes you feel better. Is Raker here or not?"

"Maybe. What do you need?"

"Nothing major. Kala told us to come here."

"Kala, huh? All right. Hang on."

The man turned around and murmured something. There was a pause. The man nodded and turned back. Without another word, he opened the door, releasing the noise. Jacob watched Xander wade into the sound. He took one last glance at the man looking down at him.

"Have fun, kid," the man said with a grin.

150

Jacob hurried after Xander.

Covering his ears against the frenzied mix of drumbeats, bass, and electronic pulses blasting from a bank of speakers over by the bar, Jacob glanced around. The whole place was like some low-ceilinged cave, bulging out in different directions. It was hard to tell how far it extended. It wasn't any brighter than the corridor outside. There were a few lamps glowing at the tables, some purple, some red, some green, but most of the light came from the tiny screens planted before the dozen or so people scattered among the tables, bathing their smiling faces in a blue glow. The men and women sat transfixed before the screens, eyes open wide, faces leaning down and in.

"What are those people doing?" Jacob asked Xander, practically screaming to even hear himself above the music.

"They're loaders," Xander shouted back. "Mostly spacers here on shore leave, looking for a little diversion. Those screens they're watching aren't normal—they grab your brain waves and pull you in. Show you whatever you want to see, or think you do anyways. I tried it once."

"What did you see?"

In the dim light, Jacob could see Xander frown. "I won't do it again," was all he said.

Jacob watched as Xander approached a man in a black robe. The man gestured to the both of them and they followed him through another door in the back of the room. Jacob breathed a sigh of relief as the door closed behind them, cutting off the sound.

His relief didn't last long. As they proceeded down a hallway toward yet another door, Jacob fell behind, his steps slowing as a wave of dizziness overcame him. It was more

151

intense than the sensation he'd felt upon waking this morning, and he had to concentrate to keep his balance, his fingers tracing along the wall as he drifted sideways. The image of Xander and the strange man in front of him blurred, shimmered, the hallway seemed to stretch out into the distance, and the sounds of their footsteps echoed in his brain. It felt as though he'd been walking forever. He paused to lean against the wall and close his eyes. *Relax*, he told himself. *You're just nervous. Everything will be fine. You're with Xander.*

He opened his eyes to discover the wave had passed and hurried to rejoin the two at the entry. The man in the black robe knocked and the door whisked open. He ushered Jacob and Xander inside.

The room was small, dark but for a small lamp on a desk across from them. Jacob froze at the sight of the man seated behind the desk. He was massive, with huge jowls that hung down the sides of his face, and his torso was so swollen that his arms, folded on the desk before him, seemed to have shrunk into his body. Strangest of all was his baby face, framed by curly red hair and sideburns.

"Good lord, Raker," Xander said, "look at you." He plopped down in one of the two chairs facing the desk. Jacob sat in the other. The man who had brought them remained by the door.

"Xander Payne," Raker said, breaking into a smile. "I knew it was you the second you walked through the door."

"So you're in the business now, huh?"

"Well, yeah. I've been at it for quite a while. Started after I left the unit. Wasn't any good as a soldier. You probably know that."

"It's been a long time."

"Too long. I still think about you, Xander, even now. I remember what you did."

"That's good, Raker. I was hoping you would. I remember you saying you owed me when I left you with the medics. I'd like to call that favor in."

"Of course, Xander. You need a job? I can always use a guy like you."

Xander shook his head. "Nothing like that. The boy and I need to visit someone. But security's likely to be tight, and I wouldn't mind having some help avoiding interruptions."

"What do you need?"

"A few cloakers would be nice. And a skeleton key if you got one."

Raker whistled and settled back in his chair. Jacob held his breath, afraid for a moment that the enormous man's mass would propel him backward onto the floor.

"I don't know, Xander. Cloakers are pretty valuable. Hard to get, you see. Worth a lot of money. A lot."

"Maybe we could work something out," Xander said, shrugging.

"Where you going that you need a cloaker, anyway?" Raker asked.

Jacob looked over at Xander, who shifted uncomfortably in his seat for a moment. "Mixel," Xander said at last. "We need to get into the tower."

Raker threw his hands up into the air. "Then there's no question," he said. "I can't let you have them, even if you could afford to pay. If you got caught, and they traced them back to me, I'd be shut down for sure."

"We won't get caught," Xander assured him.

"They all say that."

153

"Come on, Raker," Xander pushed. "You remember, don't you? Bullets, plasma bolts flying everywhere. You on the ground, bleeding, crying for help as everyone took off. And who picked you up? Who carried you all the way back?"

"You did," Raker said, looking down at his desk.

Jacob tried to imagine Xander carrying Raker's rolling mass even ten feet. It seemed impossible.

"Damn right I did," Xander said, "And let me tell you, you weren't light, even back then."

Raker looked back up. "Who is it you need to see at Mixel?"

"A friend," was all Xander said.

"That's it? A friend? What's so special about that?"

Jacob could see Xander hesitate. All along he'd been watching the exchange with a sinking feeling. He'd held off saying anything, letting Xander work it out, but he couldn't hold back anymore.

He pulled the concert ticket from the night before out of his pocket and held it flat in his palm the way he'd seen LaPerle do. Up sprang the small, glowing figure of Delaney. Raker's eyes widened at the sight of the rotating image.

"Her? I can see why you're so determined, Xander," he said, nodding. "Wait a minute," he said, looking more closely, "she's that singer, right? What are you, a fan or something?"

"Not exactly," Xander retorted. "She's an old friend of the kid's," he said, gesturing toward Jacob.

"We're like family," Jacob said. "And Mixel won't let her go. Please help us."

The image disappeared as Jacob lifted the card. "You can have this, if you want," he offered, holding the ticket out. When Raker didn't take it, Jacob put it on the desk and pushed it forward.

"Like family, huh?" Raker replied, reaching out and taking the ticket. He pulled Delaney's image back up for a moment, then put the card in his shirt pocket.

Shaking his head, Raker removed a metal tag from a chain around his neck and inserted it into a slot on his desk. A large panel in the wall behind slid open, revealing a compartment. Raker struggled from his chair, shambled over to the compartment, and removed a box. He came back to the desk and plopped down into his chair with a groan.

"Don't have a skeleton key," he said, setting the chest gingerly before him on the desk. "Not one that would work where you're going, anyway. But I know *these* beauties will."

He opened the small chest. Jacob leaned over and looked in. Embedded in a soft fabric lay six silver capsules no bigger than his thumb, a glass ring wrapped around the center of each one. Xander pulled one out and gave a low whistle.

"Pretty things, aren't they," Xander said. "Haven't seen one of these in a few years. Don't think I've ever come across ones so nicely made."

Raker nodded. "Girl on Botana makes these. A real artist." He pulled another out and handed it to Xander. "You can *borrow* these," Raker said.

"That's fine, Raker," Xander replied, taking the second capsule. "They work like any other cloaker?"

"Yeah. Just give it a twist to activate it. Should block even Mixel's sensors. As far as they're concerned, you'll be invisible. Only one catch," Raker warned. "Cloakers soak up a ton of power. Can't say how long the batteries'll last. You'll want to move quickly."

"Don't worry about that," Xander said. He stood up. Jacob did the same. "Thanks Raker," he said. "I guess we're even now."

"I'm glad I could help," Raker said. "Just don't get caught, for chrissake."

Xander looked down at Jacob. "You ready?"

"I hope so," Jacob replied.

CHAPTER FOURTEEN

Twilight was falling across the city by the time they reached Mixel Tower. The revolving door was jammed with a steady stream of workers pouring onto the sidewalk as others passed in. For a few moments they stood outside and watched. Jacob wished Xander would just hurry up and plunge in. Every second that ticked by, every second he craned back his neck and stared up at the black, glass tower stretching before him into the clouds, the more nervous he became, the more he began to believe that the venture was bound to fail. Another wave of dizziness swept over him. *Not now*, he thought. He took a few deep breaths, and the wave passed once again. It seemed like his fever was getting worse. He glanced over at Xander, who just looked down at him and winked.

"Just remember," Xander said, "this is your adventure. No matter what happens, you've brought us to this point. You're a brave one, Jacob."

Jacob nodded. As the crowd flowed around them, Xander took one of the capsules from his pocket and twisted it. Jacob heard a click and saw the glass ring light up. Xander handed the cloaker to Jacob. It was heavier than he thought it would be and warm to the touch.

"Keep it in your pocket and you'll be fine. Their sensors

won't be able to pick you out," Xander said, activating his own cloaker.

"What if Karl or somebody else sees us?"

Xander shrugged. "Not much we can do about that. Hopefully the crowd will be enough cover," he said. "Let's go."

They merged with the swarming bodies and were swept into the lobby. Jacob followed Xander as he wove his way across the marbled flooring. Instead of heading for the elevators, however, they turned toward a corridor at the far end of the main floor.

"Where are we going?" Jacob whispered.

Xander pointed to a sign above the entrance to the corridor. "Service elevator is back here. It'll be quieter."

"Won't it be more suspicious?"

"Only if somebody notices us. Anyway, look at us. We don't exactly fit in with the suits—might as well go where there are fewer people. Besides, the only ones using this elevator are the drones, and they rarely ask questions. Go ahead, press it," Xander ordered as they came to the elevator. Jacob reached with trembling fingers and pressed the up arrow, jerking his hand back as the button lit up.

"Relax," Xander assured. "You're doing fine. I told you before—this isn't life or death. It's kind of fun, actually. I always liked covert operations. Clean and quick. Mounting an assault on an orbital platform, now that's messy."

While Jacob wondered what an orbital platform was, the elevator doors whisked open and they ducked inside. Xander pressed for the seventy-sixth floor, and the elevator began its ascent with a jolt. The compartment was dimly lit; the illuminated digits above the doorway, which flashed in succession with the increasing pace of the elevator, cast as much light as the bulb in the ceiling. After a moment, Jacob could feel the compartment slow and then come to an abrupt stop.

"We're here already?" he asked Xander.

"No. We're only at twenty-five—someone else is getting on."

Jacob held his breath as the doors opened. A young man in some kind of white-and-green uniform entered the elevator pushing a cart loaded with covered dishes. A delicious aroma wafted from the tray, and a green bottle stood amid the platters. Jacob and Xander moved back to accommodate the passenger. He pressed for the sixty-ninth floor and the compartment resumed its ascent.

"Didn't expect any company," the man said. His hair was brushed low, almost covering his eyes, and he leaned forward, peering through blond strands and dim lighting to inspect the two passengers.

"Pardon?" Xander asked, as if he hadn't been paying any attention.

"This is the service elevator, that's all. The main elevators are more comfortable."

Xander ignored the statement. "Making a delivery?" he asked, lifting one of the platter covers.

"Dinner party in Suite 696. The usual. You work here too?"

"Something like that. Mixel pays the bills."

"Right. Barely, though. So what do you do?"

"You ask a lot of questions for a drone with a cart," Xander said, frowning. Jacob watched Xander step toward the man, reaching for his breast pocket where the pistol was hidden. An image of one of Turner's friends dropping on the sand at the lake flashed through Jacob's mind, followed by another of the young waiter writhing in pain on the elevator floor.

"Take it easy on him, Marshall," he said, reaching over to stay Xander's arm. "Forgive my bodyguard—he's protective. Sometimes too protective. Right, Marshall?"

Xander, looking at Jacob, smiled briefly, then turned back to the young man. "That's right—I am. It's my job, just like delivering food is yours. And when you've got the CEO's nephew to guard, you take no chances, including the main elevators. Up against the wall, please, with your arms spread wide."

The young man looked at Jacob and his jaw dropped. Then, looking at Xander, who now stood over him, he smiled and faced the wall.

"Sorry, I had no idea. Do whatever you have to do. I wasn't trying to make trouble."

"Don't worry about it," Xander reassured, patting him down. "We won't mention it if you won't."

Jacob noticed Xander slip something into his back pocket as he stepped away from the worker. A second later the elevator came to a stop and the doors opened. The young man whisked the cart into the hallway, eager to escape. When the doors had closed again, Jacob breathed a sigh of relief and Xander chuckled.

"Not bad, Blinder. You're a good little liar."

"I guess I am," Jacob said, trying to laugh.

"It occurred to me that he'd have a room service key. It'd come in handy on our trip upstairs. I was going to stun the kid, but your idea accomplished the same thing." He held up a silver card and grinned. Then his smile faded. "Jacob, are you okay?"

160

Jacob barely heard Xander as his image wavered, doubled, rejoined, and then stretched into the distance. Suddenly, he couldn't tell if Xander was dropping away or if he was the one falling.

A moment later, he came to. Xander had him propped up against the elevator wall. He could hear the man calling his name, could feel him shaking him.

"What happened?" Jacob asked.

"You tell me. You just passed out."

"I'm all right," Jacob said, struggling to his feet.

"Like hell you are. You're burning up with fever. How long have you been sick?"

"Since morning," he whispered.

Xander shook his head. "We should get out of here."

"No!" Jacob cried. He gripped Xander's arm. "We're so close. We're practically there. Trust me, I'm all right. I'm feeling better." It was partly true. The wave had passed. The ground felt solid once more. But Jacob still felt as if he were burning up. Most of all, he just wanted to lie down, curl up in a ball, and go to sleep.

A tone rang out. Xander glanced up at the lit number above the door and shook his head. The door opened and they entered the hall. It was empty. Everything was quiet.

"Guess the cloakers work," Xander said. "No welcoming committee. I'm almost disappointed."

"I'm not," Jacob said. "Come on, her room's this way."

They hurried down the hall and found her suite. Xander inserted the service key into the slot and the door whisked open. Jacob staggered by him.

"Delaney!" he cried as he rounded the corner into the suite.

The room was empty. At first, Jacob thought Delaney was just out. He'd almost expected it. But looking around the suite, he realized something was wrong.

"Her piano's gone," Jacob said, as Xander made a quick sweep of the rooms.

"The closets are empty," Xander said, returning from the bedroom. "Looks like she's been moved." He sighed and looked grimly at Jacob. "I don't know what to tell you," he said flopping onto the couch. "We could try searching some other rooms, but she could be anywhere in this place, if she's still here at all. We may be invisible to the sensors, but not to people. It'd only be a matter of time before we were caught. I'm sorry, Jacob."

In spite of how he felt, Jacob managed to smile.

"Don't be," he said. He pulled the finder from his jacket pocket, pressed the button, and spoke into it.

"Delaney Corrow."

Immediately, a beep sounded, a quick, steady pulse. He turned toward the hall outside and the sound rose in tempo and pitch.

"It's homing in on her sounder," Jacob explained. "You know, her silver pin?"

"But she doesn't have it anymore. She gave it to me, remember?"

"I returned it to her," Jacob explained. "After the concert. I thought she might want it back."

"Smart, Blinder. Very smart." Xander laughed. "After you, then." He gestured toward the door and Jacob took the lead.

They followed the finder's pulse down the corridor. A minute later it brought them to another suite on the other side of the hall. Once again, Xander inserted the service key, and the door hushed open. This time, though, Jacob didn't rush in. He paused before the door and hesitated. *Please be there*, he thought. He took a deep breath and entered.

Once again, the suite was empty. The piano was there—occupying the same spot as in the other apartment—as were her clothes in the bedroom. But Delaney was gone. The finder's pulse was almost a steady stream now. Jacob turned it off, noticing her sounder gleaming on the edge of the piano.

"She'll be back soon," Jacob said. "I know it."

"Let's hope so," Xander said. He pulled his cloaker out and examined it. The glowing ring that circled the capsule was partially dark now. "This thing's running out. Won't be long before it's drained and their sensors pick us up."

Jacob nodded and went to the window. He leaned against the sill and pressed his forehead to the pane. The glass was cool, a welcome relief against his skin. He tried to fight back the fatigue, the aching now settling into his bones, the feeling that his whole body was shutting down.

He gazed out the window to where the dying glow of sunset brooded on the horizon, enough to illuminate the sea stretching toward it. The water sparkled, just like Delaney had said.

"She wanted to be on this side," he murmured. "She wanted to be able to look out at the sea."

"Guess she got her wish," Xander said, coming to the window as the last light faded.

"I just can't believe it," the handler's voice barked as the door opened an hour later. Peering through the screen of the closet door behind which he and Xander were hiding, Jacob watched as Delaney marched into the room with LaPerle at her heels. "I mean, twice in three days? I thought we worked this out yesterday."

"I told you, I'm not feeling well. I have a terrible headache."

"I hope that's true for your sake. The whole episode was a total embarrassment; even worse than last time. You were absolutely terrible."

"Thanks," she said, throwing her sequined purse aside, groping for the couch. Finding the edge of it, she turned and collapsed into the cushions. "I'm not a machine, Jack. You can't expect me to be on at every show."

"I realize that," he replied through clenched teeth, standing over her with folded arms. "But to stop in mid-performance, right in the middle of a bloody song, and walk out like the night before? Very unprofessional. I can only do so much damage control. Your sales actually got a boost after the first fiasco, but keep this up and before long it'll be over. You'll be finished."

"I don't care," she shouted.

LaPerle crouched down in front her and placed his hands on her knees. "Don't talk that way. Does this have to do with your little friend's visit? Are you punishing me for not letting him stay the other night?"

"No, I've had a headache all day," she said, pushing his hands aside. "I haven't felt right for a few days now."

"Is it your eyes?" he demanded. She remained silent. "Well, we've scheduled an examination for tomorrow. In the meantime, think about your responsibility to us. Think carefully."

"You sound like my father," she snapped.

"I'm not your father, Delaney, but I do care about you."

He donned his smoothest tone of voice and caressed her cheek; she brushed his hand away. Listening to LaPerle's voice, Jacob shivered. Delaney was right. He *did* sound like the high councilor.

"Go away, Jack," she said. "I want to be alone."

He rose slowly and stared down at her bowed head. "Fine," he said after a moment. "I have to go back upstairs and smooth things over anyway."

Jacob watched LaPerle turn and storm out. A moment later the door hissed shut. Through the screen, he could see Delaney fall back against the sofa and press her hands to her eyes. He looked up at Xander, who only nodded in Delaney's direction and nudged him. He opened the door and stepped toward her, uncertain of his words, reluctant to disturb her. Before he could speak, she heard his footfalls and jerked her head in his direction. She gave a startled gasp and recoiled to the far end of the couch.

"Who are you?" she cried.

"Delaney, it's me," Jacob said, freezing in his tracks. "Can't you see me?"

He held up his hands as she craned forward, as if probing a distant speck. Her face relaxed at the sound of his voice, though not completely. Something was different about her from the other night, and as he returned her gaze, he suddenly realized what it was. Her eyes—they glowed, but less intensely than before.

"Jacob! Yes, I can see you now. So you decided to come back?" She smiled and beckoned him to sit beside her. "Is Xander with you?"

"Right here," Xander said, stepping out of the closet. While Jacob sat down, Xander crossed the room, going to the door to listen before settling into a chair next to them.

Jacob was about to ask her about the dimming in her eyes when she took his hand.

"I'm glad you came back, Jacob," she said. "You'll stay with me now, won't you."

"I didn't come here to stay, Delaney." He glanced over at Xander and paused. "We've come to get you out of here," he said, turning back.

She didn't reply at first. Her eyes, unchanging, unexpressive, conveyed nothing; they merely smoldered. But her smile faded. For the second time, she buried her face in her hands. Xander shook his head and, rising from his chair, went to check the door again.

"Leave?" she said, raising her head, "And go where? What good would it do? First Harmony, now Melville."

"It doesn't matter. We can worry about it later. You just seem so unhappy here."

"Why is that?" she asked. He couldn't tell if she was asking him or asking herself. Her eyes suddenly crackled, blazed bright, and then dimmed lower than before. The corners of her mouth tightened as the flickering pattern repeated itself several times.

"Delaney, your eyes!" Jacob cried, grabbing her arm. She rose from the couch and walked to the mirror with slow, deliberate steps. Jacob followed. Standing behind her, he saw her reflection in the mirror. With a dark frown, she leaned in closer until her quick breaths left moments of vapor on the surface of the glass, and her fingers probed around the metallic edges of the orbs. There was no mistaking it—the earlier glow had withdrawn, replaced by a dimness that reminded him of the dying embers of Xander's fire, their light barely

166

discernible beyond a thin layer of ash.

"It's failing," she whispered. "The vision, all of it. I'm supposed to see the surgeon in the morning, the man who planted them in my sockets when I first arrived. He removed my dead eyes and replaced them with these, but I don't know if I want him to see me." She turned from the mirror and faced both of them. "I loved them at first. They were beautiful. But now . . ."

Before she could say more, the brightness flared again, this time with a greater intensity. She screamed and covered her eyes. Tiny shafts of light shot from between her splayed fingers.

"Delaney!" Jacob shouted and reached out as she started to pitch forward. He caught her arms, made the mistake of looking up just as a voice inside told him not to, told him to let go and look away. But it was too late.

Time stopped. The room went dark, and all Jacob could see was the light shooting out of her eyes. A burning sensation ripped through him. In the distance he could hear himself wondering if it was the fever or the blue streaks of energy rolling off her and licking against his skin that made him feel like he was on fire. Most immediate, though, was the horror of recognition as his nightmare was once again made real.

No, he thought. *I'm dreaming. This isn't real. It's just the dream. I'll wake up and be back at Xander's.* But deep down, as the pain overwhelmed him, he knew it wasn't true.

Still, the last thing he heard before being swallowed up was what he always heard in his dream. A cat's voice, a distant echo of disdain:

Foolish boy, why did you return?

Through the pain, through the light, he could see its

167

golden eyes blinking in indifference.

A sudden blow struck him. He felt a moment of falling and then a thud as he hit the floor. He opened his eyes to see Xander standing over him.

"Sorry about that, Blinder," Xander said, helping Jacob to his feet. "But you were having trouble letting go. Hope I didn't hurt you."

Jacob shuddered, still foggy. "Thanks," he managed to say.

The sight of Delaney moaning on the carpet brought him to his senses. He knelt down beside her, wanting to help but hesitant to touch her again, and looked up at Xander.

"Should we call for help?" he asked.

"We have to do something," Xander replied, pulling his cloaker out. He held it up and shook it a few times. The ring was almost entirely dark. "We've only got a few minutes."

"Don't call the doctor," Delaney broke in, managing to sit up. The burning had faded and she seemed to relax slightly.

"What do you want to do?" Jacob asked, taking her hand.

"I can't stay here," she said. Her voice sounded weak but calm now.

"Fine, then let's go," Xander snapped. "Grab some clothes. I'll check the door. By the way, should we be expecting anyone?"

"I don't know," Delaney said, struggling to sit up. "The last few nights Jack's been sending Karl to check on me. They must be worried about me running away or something."

"Look's like they were right," Xander said.

"All clear." Jacob stepped into the hallway, carrying a small suitcase, and Xander followed with Delaney, who clung to him, taking meager steps. They were heading down the long,

168

curved hallway toward the main elevators when a tone chimed around the corner.

"The elevator," Delaney whispered in a frightened voice. Xander swung her around and headed in the opposite direction toward the service elevator he and Jacob had taken earlier. A moment later, rounding a corner, they reached it. Xander leaned Delaney against the wall.

"Call the elevator, Jacob. I'm going to check things out," Xander ordered. Before Jacob could beg him not to leave, the man had disappeared. Jacob pressed the button and held Delaney's hand, trying to steady himself. He felt worse than ever. He still had a fever, and having been thrust back into his dream hadn't helped. Letting go of her hand, he leaned against the wall.

"Thanks for saving me, Jacob," Delaney said, standing behind him, placing a hand on his shoulder.

"I couldn't leave you here," he said. "I had to do something."

"*I knew you would,*" she whispered in his ear.

Jacob shivered at the words, the ones he'd heard her whisper over and over in his dream the night before last. Now he knew—he had been hearing the future. He gripped the frame of the elevator doors and closed his eyes.

The doors opened as Xander reappeared, and he hurried them into the compartment.

"It was Karl, all right," Xander said as the doors closed, "and he wasn't alone. They might know something's amiss." He paused before pressing the button for the roof.

"What are you doing?" Jacob asked in alarm as the elevator began rising.

"We can't go down. In about three seconds they'll discover

she's gone and cordon off the lobby. If we can't go down, we'll go up."

"Won't we be trapped up there?" Jacob asked.

"There are floaters on the roof. I rode in one last week," Delaney offered.

"I was hoping you'd say that," Xander said as the elevator continued to rise.

A moment later it stopped. The doors opened and they stepped onto the roof. A stiff breeze pushed back Jacob's hair and made his eyes tear.

The elevator doors closed, darkening the roof. The air around the edges of the tower was sharply illuminated by the streets below. Aside from that, there was little light. Everything had shut down for the evening. No one was around.

In spite of the haziness riding in on the wave of his fever, Jacob could see a number of floaters parked across the way. They headed toward them, Jacob stumbling ahead as Xander helped Delaney along. After a dozen yards Xander simply swept her into his arms and began running as if she weighed nothing.

It seemed to take forever to cross the roof. Jacob felt as if all the energy was draining out of him with every step, and the wind did nothing to soothe the burning sensation spreading across his skin.

Don't quit, he told himself. *He has Delaney. He can't take care of you.*

Closing his eyes, Jacob forgot the pain, forgot Xander and Delaney, forgot everything and just ran.

He reached the floaters first and jumped into the back-seat of the closest one. As Xander came up and placed

Delaney in the passenger seat, a flash of light caught Jacob's eye—the elevator doors were opening.

"Someone's coming!" Jacob cried as Xander jumped into the driver's seat.

"Give me ten seconds," Xander replied, ripping out a panel at his feet. Jacob watched as three men burst from the elevator and spread out, their silhouettes fading as the doors closed. Jacob hunched down in his seat, peering over the edge of the craft, searching for the men.

"What's taking so long?" Delaney cried.

"Have to jump-start it," Xander answered. He sounded relaxed, as if all this were routine. "Don't worry, I know what I'm doing. It's just been a while."

The roof flooded with light. Jacob saw the men as they scanned the area, quickly settling their gaze in his direction.

"They see us! They're coming!" Jacob screamed as the men, banding together, stormed across the roof. He could hear them yelling orders to stop.

The men were thirty yards away when lights began blinking all across the dashboard and along the edges of the doors. A flash shot toward them from one of the men, crackling over Jacob's head; another flash struck the side of the craft, dissipating energy across its frame.

"Hang on!" Xander shouted.

The floater shuddered before jerking forward and rising into the air. Jacob watched the three figures shrink below him as they shot into the sky. Xander banked the floater hard, throwing Jacob against the side of the craft. Both Jacob and Delaney screamed and clung to their seats as the floater plunged over the edge of the roof. *This is it*, Jacob thought as Xander dove the craft down along the side of the tower before jerking it back into the normal flow of hover traffic not far above the streets.

"Sorry," Xander apologized over his shoulder. "It's been a while since I've steered a floater. They're too delicate. I'm used to the cruiser."

Both of them were too terrified to respond as Xander circled around the tower and landed the floater on the street, across from the cruiser. Crowds of people were passing by. Many of them stopped to stare, pointing to Delaney and whispering as the three of them abandoned the floater and crossed the avenue to the waiting cruiser.

They sped through the darkness without speaking, Xander pushing the cruiser nearly full throttle across the plains. Rattling in the backseat, Jacob sat next to Delaney, looking over from time to time at the dim twin sparks glowing in the darkness beside him. He asked her how she was feeling, only to realize she'd fallen asleep. He wanted to sleep too. He wanted to drift off beside her, to give in to the fever that had worked itself into a fury, but a part of him resisted. Through the burning haze, a voice told him that if he gave in, he might never wake again. So instead he stared ahead, leaning forward against the front seat behind Xander, eyes glued to the perimeter of the headlights, the tall grass a blur along the edges of their sphere of driving light. They were moving so quickly it seemed as if they would outrace the sphere of light itself and plunge into darkness.

Sleep won over near the end of their flight. One moment he was watching the path ahead cut through the sea of grass toward a point in the center of the dark and the next he was being wakened by Xander. The vibration had disappeared

172

and the cruiser was parked in the driveway. There were no moons in the sky. The night was peaceful and full of stars.

Xander lifted Delaney from the cruiser, and Jacob followed after. He dropped to the ground and walked toward the house. After a few steps, though, his legs began to wobble. He was sure they were melting, dissolving into the ground, pulling him down in the process. Before he knew it he was on the ground looking up at the stars.

The cold points of light began to spin, to twirl in circles, trace lines across the sky. The stars danced before him, and he knew that all he had to do was reach out his hand and he could touch them. But his hand was lead. It had melded with the earth that now suddenly opened beneath him, falling away and pulling him down with it. The last thing he remembered before slipping into the black was the dancing of the stars. He'd never seen anything more beautiful.

CHAPTER FIFTEEN

The chimes woke him. Jacob could hear them from outside, muffled and distant. He stretched and opened his eyes.

He saw nothing.

He bolted up in bed, gasping, gripping the blankets and pulling them up around him. He waved a hand before his face, but there was no change to the blackness around him. *I'm blind*, he thought. *It's all gone.*

Leaning toward the edge of the bed, he reached out with a fumbling hand. His fingers brushed against a wood surface. He ran his hand up its side, reached a corner, and was struck by a sudden familiarity. Lowering his head, he inhaled deeply. Yes. It was the same old smell, the same earthy dampness. He reached a little farther along the top of the bureau until his hand closed on the textured metal cube. He didn't need to open the music box to know what song it would play, to know he was back in his old room in the underground house.

He swung his legs around and got out of bed, made his way to the door, and headed down the hall, just as he had done countless times.

What am I doing here? I shouldn't be here. The words echoed in his head over and over as he made his way down the hall. Suddenly, he stopped. *But where am I supposed to be?* He couldn't remember.

He went to the front door and threw it open. The brightness of morning hurt his eyes, but a wave of relief washed over him in spite of the pain. He could see. Squinting, he gazed out into the yard and smiled. The flowers were blooming, busy with hummingbirds and insects, and the grass was green and lush. Neighbors drifted by, engaged in conversation. It was like any other morning in Harmony. He closed his eyes and drank in the sounds and smells of home.

This is real. This is my life. He had never left. He had never revealed his secret to anyone. He had considered telling his best friend Egan, but thought better of it. Why spoil a good thing?

As for last night, it was just a dream, one long dream he couldn't remember and didn't want to. He lingered in the doorway, feeling the heat of the sun on his face, sensing its brightness through the red glow of his closed lids.

A pain flashed along his temples. The glow faded, and as he opened his eyes, his smile faded too.

The bright sky had darkened. There were no clouds. Instead, a uniform gray coated the sky. He watched in dismay as the flowers in the dooryard drained of all their color, drooped, then withered into ash. Looking up, he saw the grass shriveling as well. The chimes hanging beside the door began to ring as a breeze picked up, a wind that carried the ashes of petals in a dusty cloud down the street, leaving a stubble of stalks.

Suddenly, it all came back to him—Xander, Delaney, Melville, everything that had happened since escaping Harmony, he could remember it all. He knew where he was supposed to be. But how did he get here? And how would he get back?

He left the house and ran down his street, the echo of chimes fading into the distance. Rushing into the North Tier Square, he made his way toward the fountain at its center. He felt scorched, desiccated. He needed to cleanse himself in the water, cool his body, and drink.

He had nearly reached the fountain when an odor of smoke froze him. It wasn't the smoke of a zephyr tree. It smelled more like the scent that had lingered over the toys he'd found in the basement of Xander's house. He raised his head and sniffed the breeze, trying to make sense of where the smell was coming from.

A flash in the sky caught his attention. He looked up to see a streak of red light hurtle toward earth, slanting in an arc toward the west. A moment later, there was an even brighter flash on the horizon followed by silence. The breeze died.

The quiet was short-lived. A distant boom rolled over the colony. Jacob could feel it in his chest, a wave of pressure to match the sound. Looking up into the western sky that was approaching the color of night, he saw another streak of light and then another. It was as if stars were raining from the sky.

We must be under attack, he thought. *But from whom?*

Another thought struck him as he followed the tracers of light down to the horizon. *That's where Delaney and Xander are.* How will they ever survive this? Suddenly, he was glad he was in Harmony—at least he'd have a chance.

He raced up to the fountain, noticing as he approached that its usual array of sprinklers and streams had ceased. *The power must have died again*, he thought. It had happened many times before. Gazing in, he saw the surface of the water.

Usually an impenetrable ripple of spray, it was now placid and clear.

Jacob reached down to scoop some water, when an image flashed across its surface, staying his hand. He saw Xander and Delaney huddling alone in the house with the bombs falling all around them. He could see his reflection, the shadow of his face, superimposed over their figures.

I should be there, he thought. *I belong with them.* It didn't matter if they all died. He wanted to share a final moment of life with them. How could he have been glad to be in Harmony? He was selfish. He was a Seer.

Jacob reached down and broke the surface with his hand to scatter the image. It shattered like glass, shards falling down into the basin, revealing an empty fountain. He wondered if it had always been that way.

Lifting his head he noticed the smell of smoke was stronger now. He looked around. The air had grown hazy as the sky continued to blacken. He ran to the nearest row of hillhouses, scrambled up the steep side to the top, and gasped.

A wall of flame stretched all the way across the horizon, sending thick, black smoke into the air. And it wasn't staying still. It was closing in, eating up the plain, and he knew it wouldn't be long before it would engulf Harmony, swallow everyone whole.

His heart began pounding. He felt his legs weaken. *You've got to do something,* he told himself. *You've got to warn them.* Taking a deep breath, he stumbled down off the hill and ran toward the central square.

As he ran, he kept a lookout for someone, for anyone, who could help him get the word out. But the streets were empty.

They've all left, he thought. *Maybe they found out.* But some-how he didn't think so.

Gasping for air, he hurtled down the last street toward the center of the colony. Already the acrid smoke hanging in the air had set his throat aflame. Through the haze he could make out the shapes of people as he neared the entrance. He dashed through the opening and into the square, pulling back in surprise.

A thousand faces greeted him, blank and indifferent. He had stumbled onto a Gathering. It seemed as if everyone in Harmony had collected in the square and now stood mute, waiting.

He scanned the stage. It was empty. The high councilor was nowhere in sight. He dashed over to the steps and ran up onto the platform. Recalling the last time he'd stood on this spot, it took him a moment to find his voice.

"Everybody," he called out, "you have to leave! There's a fire out there. It's coming straight for Harmony!"

No one replied. The crowd remained still. It was as if they hadn't even heard him.

"You have to believe me!" he shouted, his voice cracking. He could feel the frustration mounting within. "You're all in terrible danger!"

"Blindness is purity. Blindness is unity. Blindness is free-dom," the crowd chanted in reply.

"No!" Jacob shouted back. "You're not listening. You have to get out!"

Still, no one moved. Jacob looked around, desperate for something that could make them understand.

"Where's the high councilor?" he asked the crowd. "Shouldn't he be here?" No one replied. The sky grew even

178

darker now as the breeze continued to blow smoke closer. Jacob coughed. He had to find Delaney's father. As much as he feared and despised the man, he at least would know what to do, know how to get the people to move.

He left the stage and raced toward the high councilor's house, an aboveground concrete bunker not far away. He bounded up the steps and began banging on the door, not stopping until it finally opened and Martin Corrow stood before him.

"Fire's coming," he gasped. "Got to get everyone out."

"Jacob?" the high councilor replied. "What are you doing here? I told you when you left that you could never return."

"Who cares about that now?" Jacob cried. "Didn't you hear me? You've got to do something. Everything's going to burn!"

"I don't detect any fire." Delaney's father sniffed the air. "This is just another lie of a Seer."

"What? You can smell the smoke, can't you?" Jacob shouted. He turned and looked west. The wall of fire was closer now, casting a glow under the black sky. "And you can see it," he said, turning back. "Don't lie to me. You can see it! I know you can."

The councilor's face darkened. At last, he nodded. "You're right, Jacob. There is a fire. But it's not coming for us. It's coming for you. You're the one in danger. You came here to hide, but it found you."

"How can that be?" Jacob replied. He was so confused. It didn't make any sense, but somehow he felt that the man was right. He glanced back at the flames. "So what do I do?" he asked.

"We'll ask the ghostbox," Martin Corrow intoned. "It

179

knows everything. It will tell us what you need to do."

He strode past Jacob down the steps. Jacob followed. They hurried through the streets toward the bunker that housed the ghostbox. Before long, they'd reached the edge of the colony. From here, a stone path stretched toward the squat structure, a dark island amid the grass. Delaney's father started down the path and the two of them made their way toward the building, with Jacob stealing glances back from time to time. The fire had grown very close—it had to have reached the edge of Harmony by now. The fields must be burned, the harvest lost, and now what would the people eat? Still, looking ahead, Jacob was equally frightened. He remembered the last time he'd journeyed to the ghostbox and had faced that cold machine. Yet here he was, going back, led by the very man who'd brought him before to the room of threats and revelations.

Reaching the bunker, Jacob paused beneath the door as the high councilor waited on the other side of the threshold. Even before he looked up, he knew that he would see it. Sure enough, there the cat lay, stretched across the sill.

"You're always around," Jacob whispered. "Why don't you ever help me?"

I'm just a watcher, it replied. *You know what that's like, don't you?*

"I'm not just a watcher anymore," Jacob said.

That's true. You're changing. And you're about to change even more. Just go inside.

"I'm afraid."

Of course you are, it said. *You should be.*

"How do I know I'll come out?"

You may not. Nothing's been decided yet. It all depends.

180

"On what?"

On how strong you are.

"I don't know if I can fight."

You shouldn't. That's not how you'll get through this.

"What do you mean?"

You'll find out.

With that the cat rolled over on its back and went to sleep. Jacob started as if waking from a trance and looked around. The door before him was open. The high councilor was gone. Glancing up, he noticed the cat was gone too—he was alone. He turned back for a moment, squinting at the flames' brilliance. The fire had made its way through Harmony. He could feel its heat from here, could hear its roar as the flames twisted up into the sky, spewing pillars of smoke. Obscuring the entire colony now, it lingered at the end of the path, as if waiting for him to make the next move. He grappled with the urge to run, to tear off into the plains. But deep down he knew it would do no good. The wall of fire would follow, and he wouldn't be able to run forever. His best chance was to hole up inside and hope to make it through.

He ducked into the bunker. The doors hissed shut behind him, cutting off the roar of the fire. The room was dark except for the ambient glow of computer screens and the constellation of lights shining against the walls. In the center, rising monolithic from the floor was the ghostbox, just as he had last seen it. The yellow monocle centered near the top of the obelisk glowed brighter than the other lights, seeming to shine down on him like a spotlight, intensifying as he approached so that he nearly had to look away.

"Ghostbox," he said, hesitating. He wasn't sure what to say to it. He wasn't even sure it heard him or would answer.

"Speak," a voice said, androgynous in its reverberations.

Jacob gasped. "There is a fire coming," he said at last. "The high councilor said it was coming for me."

"He is correct."

Jacob's heart sank. Through the walls of the bunker he could hear the roar of the fire—it had reached him at last. The room was now growing warmer. He wondered how hot it would get. He gazed up at the eye.

"What can I do?" he asked.

"You can do nothing. You can only give in to it and wait. Let it do its work."

Jacob nodded. Hearing the words, he felt oddly at peace. His eyes remained fixed on the ghostbox's monocle. He couldn't have torn his gaze away if he wanted to. But he didn't want to. He wanted only to stare into the yellow light and forget all else as the walls grew hotter and the heat crept closer, licking against his skin, which now began to drip as sweat trickled down his body.

The roar now faded to a distant echo, and the eye hovering in space began to stretch out and morph. It became Delaney's eye, then his mother's. Now it was the slitted eye of the cat, now the high councilor's eye, winking its knowing wink before changing back once again to the eye of the all-knowing mainframe.

The eye was fading now as the heat reached an unbearable level. As it winked out, plunging the bunker into total darkness, Jacob knew what he had to do. He turned and walked up to the door, feeling the heat radiating from its steel. Sensing his presence, the portal slid open to reveal a world on fire, the flames now at Jacob's feet. The warmth was so intense Jacob could almost feel his body wither and burn. But he didn't wince. Instead he took a deep breath, closed his eyes, and walked into the light. Opening his eyes for a moment he could see the flames dance all around, flicker across his arms and legs, could see himself on fire. In spite of the heat, he felt no pain. He smiled and surrendered to the flames, to the fire that would somehow make him new.

Jacob!

He heard the voice. It was calling from far away, a stranger's voice, rousing him.

It was dark, just like when he'd awoken before. But this time there was no smell of earth, no sheets around him, no mattress underneath. He was floating in a void.

Jacob, look behind you, the voice called again. Like the voice of the ghostbox, it was difficult to pin down. It was a male voice, but was it young or old?

He glanced over his shoulder to see a distant pinpoint of light growing larger by the second. He had nothing to push off from, but somehow he willed himself around, hovering in place as the glowing sphere approached. Soon it loomed before him, and he basked in its light. It drew him in, enveloped him in its warmth. There was a flash as he breached the surface of the sphere and discovered ground beneath his feet. He was standing once more.

This new place was as white as the previous void had been black, with nothing around to give him any sense of perspective. He could be in a small room; he could be surrounded by infinite space. It was impossible to tell. All it was was bright.

He sensed a presence behind him and turned to see a boy standing not five feet away. He was about Jacob's age, perhaps a bit older, with a simple robe like the ones worn in Harmony only made of a rich purple cloth with gold embroidery running down the center. He smiled at Jacob and reached out a hand in greeting. Jacob tried to take it, but his own hand passed through it. He looked closer and realized the figure was shifting in and out, fading slightly then darkening, like the blades of prairie grass tossing in the wind.

"You're not really here," Jacob said.

"No," the boy replied. It was the same voice as before, modulating in pitch, giving the boy an unearthly quality. "Then again," he said, "neither are you. This place isn't real."

"Then where am I?"

"The same place I am—inside of you, inside your mind."

"Are you a part of my mind?" Jacob asked.

"Oh, no," the boy replied. "I'm merely visiting. We just found you. We sensed you were out there, but we didn't know for sure until now. And so they sent me to greet you. And to congratulate you."

"For what?"

"For surviving. You were very sick. That fever almost got you."

"The fire," Jacob said, nodding.

"Yes, the fire. You let it burn you. You stopped fighting it. And so it didn't kill you. Though it did change you."

"I don't feel any different," Jacob replied. "But it's hard to tell. There have been so many changes lately."

"Yes. But they are all tied together. The change I'm referring to started weeks ago, the fever merely accelerated it. In fact, it started the moment you began to see."

"How did you know I was blind?" Jacob asked, startled. He felt powerless. This person seemed to know all about him, but he knew nothing in return.

"Because I was too. All of us were Blinders. We are all children of the Foundation. And like you, we too began to see."

"Then I'm not alone," Jacob murmured, more to himself than to the boy.

"You've never been alone, Jacob. Even now you've got people who love you, who are taking care of you. I can sense them."

"I know," Jacob agreed, thinking about Xander and Delaney. "But I guess I meant alone in the sense of what's happened to me." He paused, gazing more intently at the boy. It seemed as if the stranger's image had blurred ever so slightly. "Did I know you back home?" he asked.

"No. I'm from a different colony. But there are a few from Harmony."

Jacob strained to hear the boy's voice, which was beginning to modulate more severely. His form began to flicker, lose its definition.

"I don't have much time left," the boy said. "I'm talking to you from very far away. From another world."

"There's so much I want to ask you," Jacob whispered.

"There's so much to tell. Gaining your vision, Jacob, was just the first step, the first change of many. Your sense of sight goes beyond what your eyes can tell you of the moment. You've had glimpses of the future already."

"The vivid dreams I've been having since I left Harmony," Jacob said. "Parts of them have come true."

"Yes," the boy said, his face now a blur. "Your first taste of what's to come. Primitive steps, but steps nonetheless."

"What comes next?" Jacob asked, the hairs rising on the back of his neck.

"It depends. It's different for all of us. But I can tell you

185

that you'll find your powers wonderful. And terrible. And strange."

Jacob could barely hear him now. "How will I recognize them?" he shouted at the flickering shadow.

"You'll know," the voice said amid the static. The modulation had grown so severe, the voice no longer seemed human. "But . . . need to learn to . . . them. . . . Want you to come to us. . . . Can show you."

"Where? Tell me where to go!" he demanded, reaching out toward what remained of the visitor.

There was a muffled ripple of sound, but Jacob could no longer make out the words as the last particles of color and shadow dissipated. He looked all around him, bewildered, hoping for a sight of the boy, but the figure was gone for good.

His disappointment was short-lived as the floor beneath him vanished. Once more he was falling, leaving the sphere of light behind, falling back into the black, suddenly too shocked and tired to care where he'd end up.

CHAPTER SIXTEEN

Jacob woke to her singing. At first he thought it was his mother, singing to him the way she always had when he was sick. A moment of panic struck him—he was back, still trapped in the dream. But then he recognized the voice. It was the voice he'd been longing to hear, low and calm, as soothing as the cool, damp cloth that lay across his forehead. For a while he said nothing. He just kept his eyes closed and listened to the song, wishing it didn't have to end.

"Delaney," he said when she finished. His own voice sounded far away and weak.

He opened his eyes and realized he was in his bed, the one Xander had given him. It was morning. The light in the window was dim, but he could see Delaney sitting beside him, could see the smile on her face, and even now her body seemed to sink slightly, relaxing in relief at his awakening.

"What happened?" Jacob asked, removing the cloth from his forehead. He remembered the ride back from Melville, remembered collapsing on the way into the house. He even had the faintest recollection of a long, strange dream— retained whiffs of it like the scent of flowers on a shifting breeze.

"Aurelian Flu. That's what Xander called it. It can be

pretty dangerous, I guess. There isn't any way to treat it. You just have to let it run its course."

"Well, how did I get it?"

"He said you could have gotten it anywhere—it's pretty common in Melville. The spacers bring it in. Most everyone has immunities against it already, so even if they come down with it, it hardly affects them."

"So why did I get it so badly?" he asked.

"I don't think they vaccinated us for it in Harmony. Since we didn't have any contact with the outside world, they probably figured there was no point. When I first came to Mixel, they gave me quite a few shots." She reached out and found his hand, squeezing it so hard he winced. He could hear the tremor in her voice. "For a while there, we didn't think you'd make it."

She leaned forward and kissed his forehead before pressing her cheek against it for a moment. "Fever's gone," she said.

"I feel okay," he replied, sitting up. His head was a little woozy, and he could hear his stomach rumble with hunger, but it felt good to be awake.

Delaney handed him a glass of amber-colored liquid. He took it, sniffed, and recoiled at the odor. It smelled worse than the medicine Xander had given him the day he'd arrived here.

"Xander wanted me to have you drink this when you awoke. It's a restorative. He mixed it himself. He said it would give you back your strength."

"I do feel a little weak," Jacob acknowledged. "Where is Xander, anyway?"

"He's sleeping. I made him go take a nap. He was up all last night."

"So I was sick all night, huh?"

"Actually, Jacob," Delaney said, "you've been unconscious for the last two days."

"What?" Jacob cried, almost spilling the drink.

"Oh, Jacob, I was so scared." Once again, her voice trembled for a moment. Then she collected herself. "Anyway, I'm glad you're back. I missed you."

"I missed you, too," he said. He downed the mixture, shuddering at the taste. Still, almost immediately, a warmth began spreading through his torso and out into his limbs. His head cleared. It was as if his whole body had been disassembled before and was now being drawn back together, stitched whole.

He turned to tell her how he felt when something caught his eye.

"You're blind, aren't you," he said, looking at her eyes. The light in them had died completely, leaving two burned-out stones, dim amid the gold rims.

She lowered her head and nodded, a thin smile crossing her lips.

"Yes," she said. "The last of it faded yesterday. It's all gone now."

The casual air in her voice surprised him—she didn't seem upset. If anything, she seemed relieved. It bothered him. On more than one occasion he had thought about how it would feel to lose his sight, to return to darkness. The thought terrified him.

"We'll take you to a doctor. We'll get them fixed," he said. "Right?"

"I like this place," she said, settling back in her chair. "It feels good to be away from Melville. All those lights. And the noise. It's quiet here, a good place to think. That's what I've been doing, Jacob. Ever since I left that tower I've been sleeping and dreaming, then waking, sitting here with you and thinking. When I dream, all I see are the lights of the city and the faces of the crowds at dinners and parties, and the keys I played on every night. It's all I ever saw. My view of the world was confined to one place and one time, and now it fills my dreams. When I woke up this morning, I heard the birds outside, the day birds. They're the same ones we have in Harmony. I woke and it was dark, but I wasn't scared. I simply rested and thought and then decided."

"What did you decide?" he asked. But he didn't want her to answer. A dark feeling swept over him. Somehow he knew he wasn't going to like what she was about to say.

"I'm going back to Harmony."

"*What?*" he cried, bolting forward. He had been half expecting her to say she was returning to Mixel. Why would anyone ever want to go back to Harmony, Delaney especially? And after everything that happened . . . what made her think she even *could* go back?

"Just hear me out, Jacob," she said. She paused for a moment before speaking. "I thought that once I left Harmony and joined the world of the Seers, life would be different. Everything would be better. I'd be free to start over. But it wasn't any better; maybe it was worse. I was just as much a prisoner, in spite of what they gave me. These eyes showed me pretty things, but they weren't enough to overpower all the other things I saw: greed, shallowness, envy, human beings clawing one another in pursuit of power, huge towers built by a company that couldn't care less about anyone, certainly not me. I got to see for myself that everything they told

190

us about the Seers back in Harmony was true."

Jacob sighed. In some ways, she was right. Closing his eyes, he again saw Turner's anger and cruelty, remembered the blows he'd received. He thought back to Coral and her friends on the beach, remembering their boredom, the jaded way they referred to their lives. But he also remembered the kindness they had shown him when, dirty and hungry, he had appeared in their midst. And then there was everything Xander had done for both of them.

"I know you haven't had an easy time, Delaney," Jacob replied, "but that's how the world is. If there's anything I've learned from seeing, that's it. Things were bad for you in Melville, but they're no better in Harmony. Our teachers always told us that Truesight allowed people to avoid the evils of the world, but you can't escape them. They're everywhere; our people just don't want to see them.

"I remember when I was brought before the council and they told me that Truesight was about embracing hardship, about being strengthened by adversity—but that's not life in Harmony. If anything, it's easier to hide behind blindness and simply pretend that because you can't see something, it doesn't exist. It just seems childish, and I don't want to be a child anymore."

"What's wrong with being childish?" she retorted. "After LaPerle and all those other creeps, I wouldn't mind being a child again. I feel so soiled. Look at my eyes, Jacob. I don't care how beautiful they are—they're not real. I feel like a monster with these circuits and wires and pieces of metal grafted into my head. In Harmony, people won't be able to see what I've become. Besides, even if you're right and Harmony is just as bad, then what does it matter whether I'm

191

here or there? At least there I'll be like everyone else. I won't be alone." She spoke with the familiar bitterness Jacob had heard so many times before, but it was strange to hear it emerge in defense of the place that had once been the object of her scorn.

"You're not alone, Delaney," he said. "I'm here, and so is Xander."

"I know," she said, softening. She reached out and touched her fingers to his cheek. "But if I stay here, I'll just be a burden to both of you. Listen, I've been thinking about this for a while, but until you showed up, I never imagined I'd have a chance to go back. I belong there, Jacob. They need me—or maybe I need them. After everything that's happened, I know I can be useful there, serve a purpose."

"But your father told everyone you were dead," Jacob said. "You can't just show up. Not without everyone knowing he lied, and he's never going to let that happen."

"I can't worry about that right now, Jacob. Father can be a harsh man," she admitted, "but I have to believe he loves me enough to find a way to set everything right." She paused. "Don't you ever think about going back?"

Jacob didn't answer. He envisioned his mother's face, smiling on the hill as the breeze swept through her hair, and his father, joking with friends on his way home from the fields.

"I'm not asking you to return with me, Jacob," she said finally when he failed to respond, "but I do need your help. Talk to Xander—he's already helped us. I'm sure he'll do it again. Talk to him. Please?"

"Why don't you ask him? You're the one who wants to go back."

"You know him better. You know the right way to ask him. I can tell how much he cares about you. He'll listen to you."

"No, I can't do it. It's crazy." He had to talk her out of it, but he needed time to think of the right words to say. For now he had to stall. "You just got out of Melville, Delaney," he said. "Give yourself some time before you make up your mind for sure, a few days at least. If you still want to go, then I'll talk to Xander. I promise."

She hesitated. "All right," she said finally.

Jacob breathed a sigh of relief and settled back into his bed. They were quiet for a moment.

"I'm hungry," he said at last.

"Xander will be up soon—he never seems to sleep long. He'll make us breakfast."

"Hope he wasn't too hard on you," Jacob joked. "He can be a bit gruff at first."

"No one's been as kind to me since I left Harmony as he has these last few days. He's a good man, Jacob. We're lucky."

"We are," he agreed.

"Grab that piece over there, will you Jacob?" Xander said, pointing.

Jacob walked over to the massive branch and grabbed on, grateful for the gloves Xander had given him to protect his hands from the sharp, rough bark. The wood was heavy, but he was still able to drag it over to the edge of the trees and lay it on the pile.

"Don't push yourself too hard, Blinder. It's only been a couple days since you came back to life. Take a break if you're tired."

"I'm feeling okay," Jacob replied, but he took his gloves

193

off anyway and sat down on the dry leaves for a rest. "That horrible drink you made me did the trick."

"Old family recipe," Xander said, laughing. "I know—it tastes bad, doesn't it?"

The shadows darkened slightly in the zephyr grove. Looking up through the branches, Jacob could see the purple clouds that had moved in over the last half hour, ushered in by a rising wind.

Earlier in the afternoon, Jacob had pestered Xander to take him for a ride. He needed to get out of that bed, that room, that house where he'd been sequestered for the last several days. As happy as he was to see Delaney again, to finally be with her at last, the awful request she'd made on his awakening—and the strange calm that had followed her ever since—had put a cloud over their time together. He had hoped that a ride on the plains might clear his head, give him a sense of how to deal with Delaney's new yearning.

Then there was the matter of the dream. The recurring nightmare that had plagued him ever since leaving Harmony finally seemed to have gone away, but there was the echo of another dream still with him, the fever-induced vision he'd experienced while unconscious in his sickbed. It lingered at the edges of his memory, palpable yet just out of reach. He wished he could recollect it—a voice inside told him it had been important, vital even.

Too many worries, too many cares, he thought. Delaney was back—wasn't it supposed to be easy now?

"How's your friend?" Xander asked, leaning against a tree across from Jacob and also taking off his gloves. They had enough wood now to fill the bed of the cruiser parked just at the edge of the grove.

"She still seems pretty tired," Jacob replied, looking away through the trees.

"She's been through a lot," Xander offered, "but she'll feel better when she's rested. You were the same way when you first got here."

"I was?" Jacob asked. He had trouble remembering. It seemed so long ago, though in reality it had been only a few weeks. "I guess I was."

"Damn straight. You've come a long way, Blinder. And I've been meaning to tell you—you did a good job back there in Melville. You kept your cool and helped your friend. Not everyone holds up under that kind of pressure."

"It wasn't that hard," Jacob said.

"No, but it wasn't that easy, either. You've got guts. Crossing the plain alone—that was hard. Hell, leaving Harmony in the first place, breaking free and leaving behind the only life you'd ever known, that was the hardest part of all."

"I don't know if I had much choice," Jacob countered.

"Sure you did. You could have submitted to the surgery and gone back to what you'd always known. Or you could have kept quiet about your sight in the first place. You could have spent the rest of your life in Harmony, living with an advantage over everyone."

"But keeping the secret, staying, even with an advantage—or maybe because of it—would have been much harder than leaving. When I told them, I took the easy way out."

"Seems like a difficult choice to me."

"It didn't *feel* difficult."

"Maybe that's because you knew you had more to lose by staying. Either way you would have lost something. Listen,

Blinder, it's not what you choose, it's *that* you choose. Choice is difficult, Jacob. What if you make the wrong one? What if you make a mistake? Not having choice, letting other people choose for you, is easy. That's why places like Harmony exist."

So what do you do if you think someone you love is making the wrong choice? "I just hope Delaney will be okay," Jacob said.

"Me too," Xander replied. "They'll figure out pretty soon what happened to her, if they haven't guessed already."

"What do you mean?"

"Mixel. They may come after us. I'd be surprised if they didn't."

Jacob's heart sank. The possibility that Mixel might come looking for Delaney hadn't even occurred to him, but now it seemed so obvious. In fact, thinking of the power contained in that black tower rushing down upon them made all of his other concerns seem suddenly trivial.

"What'll we do if they come?" Jacob asked.

"Don't worry about it. After twenty years in the muck, I know how to handle a few suits."

Jacob nodded. That was the thing he loved most about Xander—he could say things like that, and Jacob believed him.

Jacob was about to tell him so when he stiffened. A web of lightning rose within his skull, firing along the surface of his brain and down into his eyes. It was a familiar sensation— the same one he'd felt at the first awakenings of his sight well over a month ago.

The realization was short-lived as his vision blurred, then went dark. But before he even had time to be afraid, the light returned. Once again, Xander was sitting before him talking, but Jacob couldn't hear what he was saying; all he could do was marvel at how different the world around him suddenly appeared. It was as if all the colors had been drained from everything around him but for one: a monochromatic blue tinge. He tried asking Xander if he saw the same thing, but a sudden blast of wind drowned out his voice. There was a loud crack. Jacob started as an enormous limb fell from above, catching Xander across the head, knocking him to the ground and covering him with leaves. Jacob sprang forward screaming, trying to pull the limb off, but it was too late. He knew it was too late. . . .

"Sounds like a storm is coming in."

Xander's voice snapped Jacob back to the moment. He gasped and looked around. The world looked normal once again. There was a distant rumble of thunder. The sound made him shiver. He closed his eyes and tried to drive the strange, sudden image from his head.

"Suppose we could stay here," Xander said, glancing around the grove. "Enough leaves overhead to keep us dry. Probably only a passing shower anyway."

"No," Jacob said, trying to hide the urgency in his voice. A sudden impulse to get out of the grove seized him. He jumped up. "Let's load up the cruiser," he said. "I want to get back to Delaney. Come on, let's go!"

"All right. Take it easy, Jacob," Xander said, getting up. "We're not in that big of a hurry."

"Yes we are," Jacob said, grabbing Xander's arm and pulling. He didn't know what to make of the strange image that had gripped him, or the dread that had followed it. It was like his dreams, only this time he'd been awake. It didn't make sense.

197

"What the hell's gotten into you?" Xander snapped, breaking Jacob's grasp.

"I saw something," Jacob said. "A moment ago. There was wind and a branch fell and you got hurt. Really hurt."

Xander smiled and shook his head. "Oh, come on, Jacob. You need to relax. First with the dreams and now this?"

"Can we just go? Please, Xander," Jacob pleaded.

Xander sighed. "Fine. We've got enough wood anyway."

They walked out from under the trees and began pitching dead wood into the cruiser's bed.

They'd only been loading for five minutes, the thunder rolling louder from the darkening sky, when a burst of wind swept over them from the plain, followed by a crash so loud they both jumped. A moment later, the gust had faded. Jacob didn't need to look back to know what he would see. He'd already seen it.

From the edge of the grove, Xander gave a low whistle. Jacob walked over and stood beside him. Sure enough, the ground where they'd been sitting was littered with branches and leaves from the fallen limbs. It looked as if half the tree had snapped off.

Jacob glanced up to see Xander watching him with a strange, intense look. Jacob could tell he wanted to ask him about what had just happened, but the man said nothing. Perhaps he could see the look of confusion on Jacob's face, or maybe he was too shocked to speak. Either way, Jacob was glad Xander didn't ask—he didn't know what to tell him. Even now something was rising, an image in the back of his mind of a boy, someone he'd never seen before, but someone who seemed to understand him better than anybody.

They finished filling up the truck just as the rain started.

Riding back, staring out at the blurred world through the rain-coated windows, Jacob sank further and further into his seat as the fever-dream came back to him, piece by piece. Soon, he could remember it all. The strange boy's words were still echoing in his mind as they pulled into the driveway. Now, everything made sense.

CHAPTER SEVENTEEN

Two days passed. Both Jacob and Delaney continued to recover their strength, going for short walks in the fields near Xander's house or resting in the shade of the zephyr trees that filled their small valley. This evening was no exception as they climbed the hill behind the house after dinner to catch the evening breeze and listen to the birds. Reaching the top, Jacob turned to watch Xander and Delaney follow behind. Delaney was laughing—probably at some joke of Xander's, who walked beside her, guiding her by the arm. Jacob suddenly realized how good it was to hear her laugh—it was a sound he hadn't heard in a long time, even before she'd left Harmony.

Jacob dropped the rolled-up blanket he carried in the grass and plopped down on it to rest. More than anything, he wished things could stay just the way they were. Delaney had made no more mention of her desire to return to Harmony. For his part, Jacob didn't mention it either. *Maybe she's changed her mind*, he kept telling himself. Deep down, though, he knew it was only a matter of time before she would ask him again.

He was conflicted about the whole matter. He knew that it was a mistake for her to go back, but after what Xander had said about the importance of choice, he was no longer sure it would be right for him to try to stop her. A part of him wondered if any attempt to keep her here would simply be selfish on his part. After everything that had happened, he didn't want to lose her again. But, if you really loved someone, didn't you have a responsibility to keep them from making a bad decision?

The decision was made more complicated by another matter: Delaney's father. Ever since she'd expressed a yearning to go home, Jacob had been struggling over whether to tell her what he suspected about the man. The image of the high councilor winking at him in the murky light of the ghost-box chamber in those last few seconds before he'd fled kept rising before him. Shouldn't she know the truth about her father? But what was the truth? He still wasn't entirely sure. The whole thing might have been the mistake of his frightened mind. Telling her he suspected that her father could see, whether it was true or not, would change everything for her if she went back. It could even put her in danger.

Something else had begun to gnaw at the edges of his mind. He had been so intent on getting Delaney back, and had settled so quickly afterward into life with the three of them together, he'd forgotten for the moment about his own future. Even if it was, in Jacob's mind, backward, Delaney at least had an idea of where her life should go. And what about him? With Delaney gone, would he stay here with Xander forever? Even if she didn't go back, would the three of them always be together? He kept going back to the dream, to the words of that strange boy that had seemed to promise so much. He just didn't know what to make of it all.

Jacob had had no more visions since the grove and was

wondering when the next would come or if any would come at all. He'd related the vision in greater detail—along with the dream of the boy in the purple robe—to Xander and Delaney, hoping they could provide some degree of insight. Both listened with care and amazement but had little to offer in the way of understanding. The whole experience brought him back to the time when his sight had first begun to emerge: the confusion, the uncertainty, the excitement—it was all too familiar.

But all of these concerns paled against his fear of Mixel's arrival. A knot formed in his stomach every time he imagined the face of LaPerle with that plastered-on grin. It had been five days since he and Xander had infiltrated the tower and taken her away. At first, Jacob thought he would be relieved as more time went by and no one showed, but it only made him more anxious as the inevitable moment drew closer.

Xander and Delaney had now reached the top of the hill. Xander helped Jacob spread out the blanket and the three of them sat down. To the west, Jacob could make out the Melville skyline on the horizon. It looked small and contained, and all of a sudden, Mixel seemed far away. To the east, Duna—the colossal moon that wasn't really a moon—was rising visibly, its rings glittering as they caught the light of the setting sun. The breeze was cool and carried the mild scent of the prairie flowers that had recently had their second bloom. Jacob had a sudden flashback to his last birthday, when he'd shared a picnic with his parents on the grassy roof of their home. It was the first day he'd seen clearly and had been amazed watching the faces of his mother and father, seeing how their expressions had corresponded with the tone of their voices to enhance, or in some cases belie, the meaning of their words. It was then he had realized how seeing made the world a more complicated place.

"It's nice here," Xander said. "I've never really bothered to come up before."

"I missed this smell—and the song of those birds—back in the city," Delaney said.

"Let's just stay up here forever," Jacob murmured. "Keep things just the way they are." He said it as a joke, but all of them felt the truth in it.

"Everything changes, Jacob," Xander replied. "Nothing stays the same."

Jacob looked over at Delaney, who bowed her head slightly. Her smile faded.

He reached out to take her hand when the sky seemed to darken for a moment and the grass drained of all its color. This time he was more prepared as once again a flash of painful light ripped through his head and into his eyes. His surroundings disappeared and now he saw a silver craft settling down into the yard before the house. There was another flash, and suddenly he saw LaPerle taking Delaney by the arm. She was calling to Jacob, trying to pull away as Karl, his face bloody, stood over Xander, who lay in the dust nearby beside another man.

An instant later, it was over and Jacob was back with Delaney and Xander on the hilltop. They were talking and hadn't seemed to notice him. Gasping, Jacob wondered how long he had been gone. There was one thing, though, he didn't wonder about.

"They're coming," he said.

Xander and Delaney paused and looked over at him.

"What do you mean?" Delaney asked.

Before he could reply, a hum crept over the whisper of grass and evening bird songs. They all turned in the direction of the noise and saw the speck on the horizon grow larger as it approached from the direction of the city.

"Good ears, Blinder," Xander said, both of them shading their eyes to see the silhouette that had grown from a black speck to the gleaming oval of a floater. "Just when I thought they might have let it go."

"I didn't just hear it," Jacob said.

"Another vision?"

Jacob nodded. "We can't go down there."

"What do you suggest we do?"

Jacob looked around. "Can't we run away?" he asked.

"And go where? You can't always run, Jacob."

"I don't want you to get hurt," Jacob said.

Xander smiled. "I refuse to worry about what might happen. I'll leave that to you. Besides, they can't hurt me anymore."

He went to Delaney and helped her to her feet, keeping hold of her hand. Jacob joined them and took her other hand. She was trembling slightly as the hum grew louder. Jacob squeezed her hand reassuringly, and a brief smile flickered across her face. Comforting her was the only thing that alleviated his own fear.

The floater glided down and landed in the driveway near Xander's cruiser. From the hilltop Jacob could see that Karl steered the craft, his massive bulk filling the driver's seat. LaPerle and another man even larger than Karl were seated in the back. The three got out and lingered in the yard, waiting.

"Guess we better go see what they want," Xander joked. Delaney gave a nervous laugh. Jacob wished he could laugh also, but his stomach was too tied up in knots.

The three of them took their time going down the hill, catching the last rays of the sun before it slipped down over the horizon as they came from behind the house and into the yard.

"Nice little place you have here," LaPerle called out as the three approached, coming up to stand beside the cruiser. Xander said nothing. He simply leaned against the cruiser with his arms folded.

"I get it—the strong-silent-type routine. Is that what she's looking for?" LaPerle sneered.

Xander ignored the question. "What took you so long?" he asked instead.

"Business, the usual. Besides, I figured she'd return on her own. After all, look around—not quite the luxury we've provided. Look, I don't want to spend any more time out here in the bush than I have to, so let her go and we'll be on our way."

"Unlike you, I'm not keeping her here. She just doesn't want to go back."

"Doesn't she? That's for her to say."

"He's right, Jack," Delaney said, stepping forward. "I'm not going back."

"It's not that simple, Delaney," LaPerle stated. "We've invested a considerable sum in you. You owe us."

"I'm not an investment. Besides, the eyes don't even work. They've caused me more pain than they're worth."

"Blind again? I told you before—implants can be tricky. If you'd allowed the surgeon to make the right adjustments, you'd be fine right now. Delaney, we can make this work. Stop being ungrateful."

"Don't worry, I'm plenty grateful for everything these eyes have shown me," she said.

LaPerle either didn't understand the sarcasm or chose to ignore it. "Then start acting like it. Besides, think of all your fans. Think of what you're doing to them. They miss you, Delaney. Your last couple screwups haven't hurt you. Believe it or not, it's made you more popular than ever. We're getting inquiries from all over the Rim. People want to know the truth behind the mystery."

"Well, I'm going to have to disappoint them," she replied. "I don't care about any of that. I thought I would at first, but I don't. All I can think about is what I've done to myself. And I don't like it. I don't want that life. I'm sorry."

"What's this guy filled your head with, anyway? Whatever he's offering you, I can offer you far more. You know that."

"You just don't get it. It isn't what's offered, Jack, it's what's demanded, and he hasn't demanded anything. He's the *only* one who hasn't."

"All right, enough of this banter," LaPerle said in a bored tone. He turned back and nodded to the giant beside Karl, who stepped up. LaPerle snapped his fingers and gestured toward Delaney.

Jacob darted forward to stand in front of her. Xander continued to lean against the cruiser but stared intently at the man. As he approached, the man fixed his gaze on Xander in return, puzzled at the other's passivity. Xander never wavered as the man drew near, but it didn't matter—one second Xander was leaning, the next he was a blur, springing before anyone could react.

He caught the giant with a chop to the throat, and the

206

man fell to his knees, gasping with one hand on the ground, the other at his neck. In spite of his terror, Jacob felt an instant of relief to see the man go down. But as Xander closed in to finish him off, the man lashed out, swinging his massive arm in an arc that caught Xander in the face, knocking him backward onto the ground. Jacob watched in horror as Xander struggled to pick himself up. The man loomed over him, as if daring him to rise, too distracted to notice Jacob, who, bending down, scooped a handful of sand from the driveway and threw it in the giant's face. Blinded, the man cried out and retreated, bringing both hands to his face. His stumbling gave Xander enough time to recover and lunge forward. He drove his fist into the man's stomach, following it with a series of blows. With a grunt, the man dropped into the dirt as if he had been struck with a stunner.

Breathing hard, Xander pulled himself erect and straightened his shirt. Blood ran out of the corner of his mouth. LaPerle, not moving from his original position, just sighed and, looking down at the man, shook his head in disgust.

"Very nice, Mr. Payne," he said to Xander, "but like I told you once before—don't think you can bite the hand that feeds you any more than our young lady friend here can. I don't care what you've done for us or what you've gone through in the process; if you don't step aside, we'll cut you off completely. No more pension, your land rights will be revoked, and you'll be shipped out to space. How's that for a deal?"

Xander had now caught his breath and was smiling, as if he had been waiting for this threat all along. "You want a deal? Fine, I've got one for you. For over ten years I fought for MixelCorp. That's a long time to do someone's dirty work, and believe me, I did enough of it and saw even more. A long time ago, I realized that it might be smart to keep records of everything I'd done and seen—call them memoirs, if you like. I finished them just last year and sent them somewhere special, somewhere secret, where even Mixel can't find them. So here's my deal: you back off and maybe I won't publish those memoirs after all."

"You're lying," LaPerle said, his eyes narrowing.

"I might be. Investigations, inquiries, fines and bad publicity—those are all ugly words to have to hear just to find out if I'm telling the truth. Look, *Jack*, I may be a mere soldier, but I've spent enough time in the company of suits to know that it all comes down to the bottom line. I don't care how much you've put into this young lady—you and I both know it isn't worth it. Especially to you."

LaPerle didn't respond for a minute. He only stared at Xander, trying to glean any hint of the truth from the man's blank face.

"A ridiculous bluff," he said at last. He turned back to Karl. "Karl, I guess it's up to you to do the honors," he said.

Jacob watched as Karl stepped forward, a dark look on his face. The memory of his vision flashed through his mind. He knew he had to do something fast. He ran forward and stepped in front of Xander.

"Don't, Karl! Please," he shouted. Karl pulled up in surprise and stared down at Jacob, frowning. Everyone was quiet. Jacob realized all eyes were on him.

"You don't want to do this," he continued. "I know you don't. Xander's told me what the two of you went through. Back in Melville you said that it was just business, but you know that's not true. This isn't just business."

Karl's frown deepened as he looked over at Xander, who simply looked back and shrugged. Finally, he shook his head and turned back. While Jacob breathed a sigh of relief, LaPerle gave the passing man a dark look.

"What're you doing?" he snarled.

Karl shrugged his shoulders. "Can't do it," he said. "Kid's right."

"You want to keep your job?"

"Yeah, I do. But not this way. Besides, you should believe Xander about those memoirs—I used to see him writing all the time. We all did."

LaPerle stared at both men for a moment in disbelief. "Isn't anybody loyal these days?" he shouted at last. He turned and kicked the ground, sending up a small dust cloud along with a string of obscenities. By the time he turned back, he had regained his composure.

"Get up, you idiot," he said to the giant, who only now was beginning to pick himself up off the ground. "We're leaving. I have a meeting in an hour."

With another groan, the man rose and, brushing the sand off his suit, limped back to the floater with Karl and LaPerle. The three of them got in. LaPerle never looked at Xander or Jacob as he settled into the floater that had already begun rising off the ground. A minute later it disappeared from view.

Jacob ran over to Xander, who now leaned back against the cruiser, rubbing his jaw and spitting out saliva mixed with blood.

"Are you okay?" he asked.

"I'm fine. Good move back there. You really covered me," Xander said, reaching out and squeezing Jacob's shoulder. Delaney joined them, her hands groping until she found Xander. She felt along his shoulders to his face, drawing her hand away when he winced as she brushed his cheek.

"You're hurt," she observed.

"Just like old times," he joked. "Nothing like a good blow to the head to make you feel alive."

"Xander—" she began before he interrupted.

"Don't thank me. It was worth it just to ruffle his feathers a bit."

"Did you really mean it?" Jacob asked. "Do you really have all that stuff written down?"

Xander shrugged his shoulders and smiled. "Why spoil the surprise?" he quipped.

This time all three of them laughed.

"You'd better get some ice for your face," Delaney said.

"Right," Xander grunted.

He turned and went inside. Jacob turned to follow when Delaney stopped him.

"Jacob," she whispered.

His heart sank hearing the quiet sound of his name, but he turned back to her. She reached for him, and pulled him in close.

"Is he gone?" she asked.

"Yes."

She leaned in, her voice soft but intent. "You have to ask him. Tonight. You promised me you would."

"But it's only been a few days. Can't you wait a couple more before you decide?" he pleaded.

"I'm not going to change my mind, Jacob. You know I won't. And what just happened has given me an even bigger reason to leave. I need to get away from Mixel for good, for your sakes as well as mine. If there's one place they can never touch me, it's Harmony."

"But you don't need to worry about them anymore. You heard what everyone said. You heard what happened. It's over."

"I didn't hear that, Jacob. LaPerle never said it was over, did he?"

Jacob couldn't remember hearing the words. Still, he didn't want to give in.

Delaney sighed. "Maybe it is, maybe it isn't. I don't want to take that chance, Jacob. Trust me, I know what I'm doing."

"No, you don't," he replied, his voice rising. Before he could stop himself, the words rushed out. "You're just doing this because you're desperate, because you don't think you have any other choice. This is just like you, Delaney. Everything has to be taken to the extreme. Back in Harmony it was the same way. I don't think you'll be satisfied no matter what you do. At least if you stay here, you'll make me happy. You'll make Xander happy. Doesn't that matter?"

For a moment, they were both silent. Jacob searched Delaney's face, afraid of what her reaction might be. But to his surprise, she seemed to give no reaction at all.

"I'm sorry, Delaney," he whispered. "I just don't want to lose you again. After everything that's happened."

"You don't want me, Jacob," she said. "I'm broken. An outcast."

"We all are, Delaney. Xander, me, you. None of us fit. That's why we belong together. Why can't you see that?" He winced as soon as he finished saying the words. She reached up to touch her jeweled eyes and gave a flicker of a smile.

"Listen to you," she said. "You sound so grown up. Thinking back to all those afternoons we spent together in Harmony makes me realize how much you've changed. I wish I were as strong as you."

"You are, Delaney."

She shook her head and sighed.

211

"You might be right, Jacob. All those things you said about me before—they're probably true. But I still feel like I have to try this. It's my decision, after all. Isn't it?"

"Yes," Jacob said. He thought about going home, what it would be like. In some ways, it felt like he already had. An image of his mother, seated at the table with his music box, mourning, rose before his eyes, a memory from one of his earlier dreams.

"I'll talk to Xander," he said at last.

CHAPTER EIGHTEEN

Jacob stepped into the firelight and occupied his customary spot across from Xander, who looked up before returning his gaze to the flames. The man threw a log into the pit and followed the flaring sparks until, having exhausted their own energy, they disappeared.

"How's Delaney holding up?" Xander asked.

"She's all right."

"Hope that scene didn't rattle her too much," the man said, bringing a hand up to touch the swollen side of his face.

"She's scared they'll come back."

Xander shook his head. "I don't think they will. It's over."

"That's what I told her," Jacob said.

For a few minutes, they were silent as Jacob worked up the courage to speak. He'd spent the last hour pondering how to convey Delaney's wish to Xander. And in that time, thinking about his own future, another idea had gathered in his mind. Now, he had his own request to make. He looked up at Xander.

"I had an interesting talk with Delaney earlier," he said, trying to keep his voice from shaking. "She wants to return to Harmony. She wants you to take us back."

Jacob held his breath, wondering how Xander would

213

respond. The man didn't speak for a moment, but in the dim light Jacob could see his eyes narrow and the creases of his face deepen as he frowned.

"You can't be serious," he said at last. "I know she had a bad experience in Melville, but what makes you think she'll be any better off in Harmony?"

"I don't understand it either, but she's made up her mind."

"Besides, didn't she run away? Why would they take her back?"

"No one knew she left. Her father told people she was dead."

"All the more reason. And you said 'us'—'take *us* back.' Don't tell me you're going with her?"

"I am," Jacob said. "But not to stay," he added as Xander's scowl deepened. "Ever since I began to see, I've been trying to understand my place in the world, who I am. And my dreams and visions have only made the feeling grow stronger. I want to know why all this has happened to me. I want to know what I'm supposed to do. The only place I can think of to start looking is back where it all began. I don't know what my future's going to be, but maybe going back is a good place to find out."

"Oh, really? And what are you going to do? Walk up to Delaney's father and ask him to tell you what he knows?"

"Maybe," Jacob retorted. "I don't know right now, but I'll think of something. Someone there must know the truth. After all, the boy in my dream said there had been others like me from Harmony."

"Go back to move forward?" Xander said, shaking his head. "I don't buy it, Blinder. You have to accept the truth—

they're not going to help you. They don't want anything to do with you, at least not the way you are. You're a Seer to them now and always will be. Even if they had blinded you again, they would've always thought of you that way. And what if they keep you there, throw you to the ghost machine, or whatever you called it? It's dangerous, Jacob."

"I have to try," Jacob replied. "Otherwise I'm just running away, like I did before, only this time for good." He suddenly realized how much he sounded like Delaney. For the first time he felt like he understood her. "Besides, didn't you say back when I first arrived that the problem with Harmony is that they're running away, rejecting the truth of life's pain?"

"That's different," Xander growled.

"I don't know, maybe it is. All I know is that there are others out there like me, and I'm going to find out about them if I can. As for Delaney, she'll never change her mind—she's too strong-willed."

"Maybe that's why she escaped in the first place, or has she forgotten that? Besides, don't forget that you're depending on me to get the two of you there. She sure as hell can't make it herself on foot in her shape, even with your help. Suppose I refuse to take you back? In fact, why should I?"

"Because it's her decision and mine. Remember what you said before about choices—even bad ones."

The fire had burned down and darkness was encroaching. All Jacob could see of Xander now was his glittering eyes. He tried to imagine what those eyes had seen.

"Maybe I'll help you and maybe I won't. We'll have to wait and see. If I do, it won't be for a while."

"That's fine, Xander."

"Don't get too excited. A lot can happen. Despite what

215

you said, she might change her mind. Remember, she's come from a tough place and anything looks good right now, even Harmony. Now that she's blind again, maybe for good, her old life probably looks even better. But in a few days, after things settle down and she becomes stronger, she'll remember her reason for escaping in the first place."

He stood up and kicked some sand onto the coals, darkening the circle.

"Maybe you're right," Jacob said, standing up to join him. But he knew he wasn't.

The next morning, Jacob found himself being shaken awake. He sat up from the sleeping pad and blankets he'd used since giving Delaney his bed and looked out the window of the room they shared. The sky was early gray.

"So did you ask him?" Delaney said, kneeling on the floor beside Jacob.

"What time is it?" Jacob asked, yawning.

"I don't know, but the birds started calling at least a half hour ago. I hardly slept last night. So did you ask him or not?"

"Yes," Jacob replied. "He said he'd think about it."

"But he didn't say no?"

"No." Jacob didn't add what Xander had said about the idea.

She smiled. "Good. That's good. He'll do it, Jacob. I know he will."

"He said that even if he did, it wouldn't be for a while," Jacob warned.

"That's okay. We'll give him time. That's all he needs."

Jacob lay back on the pad and listened to the morning birds outside. "Delaney," he said at last, "have you ever visited the ghostbox?"

216

After talking to Xander, he'd spent the rest of the night trying to think of who might know about the changes that were happening to him. The only person he could think of to ask was the high councilor, but Jacob didn't see how the man would be willing to tell him anything, nor did Jacob feel like ever facing him again. Maybe one of the other councilors would know something. He thought of tracking down his friend Egan's father, Mr. Spencer, or perhaps Sonya Donato, the councilor from his own neighborhood, but it all seemed too risky. How could he trust any of them?

Then he suddenly remembered a moment from his dream when—with the flames encroaching—he'd hurried to the high councilor's door and asked him for help.

We'll ask the ghostbox, the man had said. *It knows every-thing. It will tell us what you need to do.*

"Sure," Delaney said. "I used to sneak over there from time to time. It was a nice cool, quiet spot to hide from Father and everyone else."

Jacob was relieved. The bunker that contained the ghost-box was strictly off limits to the citizens of Harmony, but Jacob figured if anyone had broken that rule, it would have been Delaney. "Did you actually talk to it?" he asked.

Delaney nodded. "It was a good listener. It didn't scold or judge. Of course it didn't have too much to offer in the way of advice, but now and then it would surprise me."

"Weren't you worried it would tell your father?" he asked.

"It never seemed to have told him I was even there," she said, shaking her head. "I don't think it really cared. It just did its job and minded its own business."

"Then maybe it doesn't know anything after all," Jacob murmured. He told Delaney about his plan, his hope that

217

maybe he could find out more about what the boy from his dream had told him.

"My father told me once that it was linked to the Foundation's mainframe back on Earth. If there are secrets in Harmony or the Foundation, the ghostbox probably knows them," she said.

"I wonder if it would tell me anything. It must be protected."

"The building is locked. But I know where Father keeps his key. When we go back, I'll get it for you. Once you're inside, you should be okay. I think you just need to know the right questions to ask."

Though her eyes remained two dead stones, Delaney's spirit grew brighter by the day as her strength returned. To Jacob, her decision to go back seemed to be the source of this lightening, which fed his own desire to return, his hope of finding a clue to the nature of his visions.

A week went by. Then another. Another followed that, and still none of them spoke of the return. But it was there, hanging over every meal, over every walk they took together with Jacob and Xander guiding the young woman on either side, over every evening when Xander would read to them from one of his books. It didn't seem to dampen the time they spent in each other's company, at least in Jacob's mind. If anything, it made him cherish it more. Jacob thought the feeling was true for all of them, including Xander, maybe Xander most of all.

He'd told Jacob how much Jacob had changed since first coming to live at the house, but if anyone had changed it was Xander, especially since Delaney's arrival. Jacob noticed how much lighter he seemed in the mornings, how he spoke more often and with less bitterness in his voice. At first, Jacob had been nervous of the man's volatility, the sudden and unpredictable mood swings that would drive Xander out into the plains for long rides in his cruiser. The solitary excursions were rare now. Jacob wondered if all that would change with Delaney's departure. So far, Xander had given no indication of his intent, but Jacob felt it was only a matter of time before he acquiesced to Delaney's request.

Maybe today will be the day, Jacob thought as he floated on his back in the water, staring up at the afternoon sky.

As he had every day for the last several weeks, Jacob had spent the morning learning to read. With Xander's help he'd made quick progress. Already he knew the alphabet and the different sounds its letters made. He could read many basic words. He'd even managed to read by himself most of the first poem Kala had given him at their first meeting—a simple song about a lamb.

To celebrate, after lunch they'd driven out to the same lake where Xander had rescued Jacob weeks ago. It was strange for Jacob to return to the place he'd first made contact with the world beyond his old life. He half expected to see himself still there, a little boy ghost, hungry and ragged, but all signs of his earlier visit had been erased; it was as if no one had ever been there at all. The sands had been blown clean, and the water was clear and striking beneath the sun.

For the first time in his life, Jacob swam. Waist-deep in the warm water, Xander showed him how to float and how to hold his breath, and he taught him a few basic strokes. Delaney waded in too, her blindness causing her to step with slow grace to midthigh. Her dress floated out on all sides as she dipped her fingers in the water.

Though Xander and Delaney soon tired of the water and left to sit on the hillside overlooking the lake, Jacob remained. Again and again he pushed himself over the surface, gliding with his head down, relishing the sensation. After a half dozen times, he dared to open his eyes under water as he floated and marveled at the hazy blue that deepened on the horizon until it was nearly black against the plain of sand below him. The water stung his eyes at first, but he became accustomed to it, and soon the pain was obscured by a wonder of the underwater world in which the pale skin of his hands seemed to acquire a transfigured glow. Bubbles plucked from the surface curled around his fingers, tickling his skin on their return trip.

But he loved floating on his back most of all. It took Xander a good hour to teach him how to spread his arms and legs out, tilt back his head, relax his whole body, and let go. That was the best part. The sensation of floating was wonderful, but forcing himself to calm down, to unclench his whole body, was an even more welcome experience. He hadn't been this at ease since before he'd recovered his sight, maybe never.

Now he closed his eyes, felt the water close over his face until only his nose remained above the surface. The world was quiet underneath. All he could hear was his breathing and—when he went totally still—his heartbeat. He felt his mind spin, roll up into itself, and it seemed as if his body was following along, turning somersaults in the water. It felt like he was drifting away. . . .

Jacob opened his drowsy eyes and gazed in wonder. He was up on the hill overlooking the lake. Before him Delaney and Xander were sitting in the grass. He turned his head slowly, confused by his surroundings.

How did I get here? he wondered. He couldn't remember leaving the lake. He had been in the water. He had been floating. He shielded his eyes and stared down at the lake, down to where he still floated.

There I am, he thought. *How strange.* Somehow he thought that this new aspect of his emerging sense of sight should bother him—to be detached, to be two places at once—but it didn't. Perhaps it was due to the drowsy lull that hung about his head, the feeling of relaxation that seemed so alien in its comfort. Or perhaps it was because it just felt right being here, together with the two people who accepted him for who he was. He flopped down in the grass behind the couple. They didn't turn to say hello or even seem to notice him—he was invisible. They just continued their conversation. He lay back in the sun on his side, watched, and listened.

"I don't think he'll ever stop," Xander said to Delaney.

"What's he doing now?" she asked, and Xander shaded his eyes, looking below at the boy in the water.

"Oh, he's just playing around, floating on his back."

"I'm glad he's having fun," she said. "He is still a boy, after all, despite what's happened."

Delaney lay back against the hillside. Like her dress in the water earlier, her long black hair fanned out on all sides, and for a moment it looked as if she, too, were floating.

"I can feel the sun on my face," she said, "and the wind bringing the scent of those trees up the hill from along the water's edge. What did you call them?"

"Zephyr trees."

"Right. We don't have them in Harmony. We should." She smiled. "Tell me what you see," she said.

"I don't need to. You've already described it. Besides, that's what poets do. I'm no poet."

A hawk flew over them from the ridge, its shadow flickering across Jacob's eyes for a brief second as it soared away from them, maintaining an almost even plane with their position on the hill before diving and gliding across the water and into the darkness of the trees on the opposite side.

"Jacob told me what happened to your family," she said after a moment. "I'm sorry. Our suffering is nothing next to yours."

"Everyone's suffering is different, but pain is pain," Xander said. "We all deal with it in our own way, don't we? Even if it doesn't always make sense."

"Yes," Delaney said, pausing. "I want to thank you for everything you've done for Jacob and me. With the others, there was always an expectation, a price. You've asked for nothing in return."

Jacob watched Xander gaze down at her for a moment, at the lines of gold that rimmed the pale crystals, at the blades of grass that sprouted between her hair, before turning away.

"I don't feel the need," the man replied.

"You've done so much, and that's why I know you'll help us again. You'll bring me back," she said.

He was quiet a long time. "After tomorrow," he said at last, and then lay back in the grass.

One more day, Jacob thought.

"I still think it's a bad idea," Xander continued. "In fact, I don't understand it at all."

"I'm a Blinder. I was before and now I am again. Where else would I go?"

"But you ran away. You've been declared dead by your own father, all because he couldn't tell them the truth. Why? Because he was ashamed? Because if you left openly, others might want to leave also? Even if he does take you back, returning will just reinforce everything they already believe about the world and play right into his hands."

"I'm aware of the problems involved here. I remember what it was like, what it has always been like. But things change. Maybe if I return and he's forced to explain what happened, things *will* change. A good dose of truth never hurt anyone."

Xander laughed. "You're too innocent for your own good. People don't change easily, if ever. Asking your father to admit a lie and expecting everyone else to suddenly understand that it's just the first of many lies and half truths is as cruel as . . ." He stumbled for an analogy. Delaney stepped in.

"As cruel as a Blinder suddenly being able to see?" she asked.

He remained silent, turning away to look down at Jacob still floating in the water.

"You don't have to go," he said after a moment, and this time she was silent.

The next day flew by. Jacob tried to make it pass slowly, taking notice of each moment, and at times it worked. Then something would happen and he'd lose his concentration and before he knew it an hour had passed or maybe two. Now it was evening and they were gathered around the fire. Delaney had joined them tonight, one of the few occasions she'd made it down. As before, Xander had given her his seat—a smooth, flat stone—to sit on.

They were quiet. The stream of conversation, which usually flowed so quickly, had slowed to a trickle at dinner as they shared their last meal together. Now, each seemed content to listen to the cracking of the wood as the fire took each piece and to smell the fragrant scent of the zephyr's smoke.

"When do we leave?" Jacob asked.

"Early," Xander said. "If we head out in a few hours, we can be there by dawn."

"It'll be quiet then," Delaney said.

"That's what I'm hoping," Xander replied.

The silence resumed. Finally, Delaney spoke up.

"What do you think, Jacob? Shall we do it now?"

"Okay," Jacob said. As Xander looked on in confusion, Jacob got up and went behind a tree, returning with a bag. He pulled out the small harp and the whistle. Xander started at the sight of the instruments. Jacob walked over to Delaney, put the harp into her hands and, still standing beside her, turned to face Xander.

"Jacob took these from the trunk in the basement," Delaney said. "He told me where they came from. I hope you don't mind."

"No," Xander rasped.

"I'm glad. We wanted to do something to thank you for saving both of us on the plains, for rescuing me from Mixel, for giving us a place to stay. For everything you've done for us. We'd like to play you an old song from Harmony, something Jacob and I can both play. It's one of our favorites."

Xander shifted in his seat. Jacob could tell he seemed uncomfortable, but he nodded his thanks.

Delaney started first, plucking each of the little strings in succession before settling into the melody. A minute later

Jacob joined in, adding the breathy notes of the whistle to her strings. The song began slow, almost mournful, and Jacob watched as Xander looked away from them and down into the fire, his hands clasped before his mouth. Delaney's fingers danced along the strings, moving effortlessly as she wove the intricate layer of tones into a steady and seamless pattern.

As he played along, Jacob realized he'd never felt so close to her. It was as if the sound each of them created stretched toward the other, wound together into a single cord that could never be broken, and for the first time he felt at peace with the idea of her leaving—at least this moment, this song, would be with him always. It was then he realized that this performance was as much for his sake as it was for Xander's, maybe even more for him, though Delaney had never said so.

The song shifted now, picked up in tempo, grew lighter as it pushed toward the finale. This was Jacob's favorite part. He stopped watching Xander, forgot about Delaney and her leaving, and focused solely on the rapid fingering of the tune. The mourning had left the song and become joy. He could feel it wash over him like the warm water of the lake. He had practiced the song many times before, both in Harmony and with Delaney over the last couple of days, but he had never played it this fast before, or with such precision.

The song ended with a succession of quick strums against the strings and a final trill of the whistle. Jacob, realizing he had closed his eyes somewhere along the way, opened them to see Xander smiling broader than he'd ever seen. The man clapped and laughed, as if in spite of himself.

"Amazing," he cried. "I liked that last part especially. You can't help but feel good listening to it."

"That's the idea, I think," Delaney said.

"Who would've imagined that little harp could sound so good. It's just a child's toy, really," Xander said.

"I spent some time this week tuning it. It's a nice little piece."

"It is," Xander said. Jacob saw his face fall for a moment. "That first part," he said, "the slow one. It was so sad. What's it supposed to be about?"

"Whatever you want it to be," she said.

Xander nodded. For several minutes the song's presence remained with them, hovering about their ears and over the fire between them.

"You two had better turn in," he said at last. "Be good for you to get at least a little sleep before we take off."

Jacob helped Delaney up and the two of them started out. Reaching the mouth of the path, Jacob looked back. Xander was still seated by the flames. Jacob watched as he pitched another log onto the fire. Then he turned and led Delaney onto the path toward the distant lights of the house.

It was dark when Xander woke them. They rose, silent in the cool night, gathered Delaney's few belongings, and headed out to the cruiser. Jacob looked up at the pink moon as they crossed the yard, a slim crescent in the eastern sky, hovering over their destination.

Jacob helped Delaney into the backseat while Xander fired up the engine. A minute later they'd left the valley, climbed the nearest hill, and were heading east where there were no roads.

CHAPTER NINETEEN

Jacob watched the pink moon slip through the crack of sky that shone between cloud and horizon, surrendering to the half light that had begun to gather over everything. In the predawn no color appeared, merely textures of light and dark. Xander and Delaney were forms of gray, almost indistinguishable from the cruiser behind them. It should have been brighter, but a blanket of clouds muted the sky, and a sudden stir of breezes, unusual for the morning, hinted that a storm was rolling in.

From their spot on the ridge, Jacob could barely distinguish the emerging shape of the colony below. When he was blind, it had seemed so large, stretching among the rises in the darkness of his perception. It had grown smaller as his sight defined its borders. Now, after having crossed the plains and navigated the streets of Melville, it seemed smaller still.

"We'd better go," he said, as much to himself as to Delaney. All night, plunging through the darkness, Jacob had been stirred by that same mix of apprehension and excitement he'd felt on the approach to Melville to rescue Delaney. And now here they were, preparing to deliver her back to the one place he'd never thought he'd return.

They had arrived less than an hour ago, stopping only

once to eat and to stretch their legs. Then they had waited; they would enter the colony when Jacob could see enough to lead Delaney, but before the day had begun in earnest and people had left for their duties. In another hour, the workers in the fields would be relieved by the next shift. Jacob wondered if his father was there right now, busy with the labor of preparing the land for the next planting.

"Jacob's right. You'd best be going," Xander said, handing over her bag. Delaney embraced him quickly and whispered her thanks in his ear.

"I know," he said. "I just hope it turns out the way you've imagined."

She left Xander and reached for Jacob's hand. He took it, and they walked down the hill.

"I'll see you soon," Jacob called back.

"I'll be waiting," Xander replied, adding, "you've got an hour, Blinder. Then I come looking."

It seemed to take forever to make their way into Harmony. The entire time he kept imagining standing before the ghostbox, kept seeing that glowing eye.

In the dim light the colony seemed alien and unfamiliar. Though he had walked these streets his entire life, he felt disoriented. He knew where Delaney lived, but it took him several attempts to find the correct path to the high councilor's quarters. On the way they passed several citizens out early in preparation for the day. Each time, Jacob squeezed Delaney's hand and they froze, afraid that the slightest footstep might reveal their presence, but each time, the person simply walked past them, unaware. Finally, they arrived at the house—a concrete block close to the council chamber in the heart of the community.

Jacob opened the front door and they entered, closing it silently behind them. Delaney disappeared before his eyes as the darkness swallowed them. He felt her take his hands and draw him near her. Jacob realized that he had to say good-bye.

"Where is he?" Jacob whispered.

"He's probably still sleeping. The bedroom's just down this hall," she said, sounding far away in the dark. Her hands were steady in his grip, but her voice trembled, and he could hear her breath quicken. "Stay here," she whispered. "I'll be right back."

Before he could say anything, she let go of him and was gone. A minute later she returned and pressed a small card into his hand. "Here's the key."

"Thanks," he said, and then paused. "Well, this is it, I guess."

"Yeah, I guess it is," she said. "Good luck with the ghost-box, Jacob. I hope you find what you're looking for."

"I just hope you'll be okay," Jacob replied.

"I'll be fine. I really will. He'll be glad to have me back— I'm his daughter. Right?"

"Right," he said. "I'll miss you, Delaney."

She drew him into her arms and kissed him on the fore-head. "You'll see me again someday. I feel it. Who knows, maybe you'll come back too. Everything could change," she said.

It already has, he thought.

"Wish me luck," she whispered and released him to the dark.

He heard her walk away, her steps fading as she turned a corner. It was her house. She knew where she was going. He reached out before him, turning in the pitch-black, taking slow steps until he reached the wall, tracing his hand along it to the door. His fingers were on the latch when he stopped, gasping as a new light absorbed the darkness.

It started with a flash in his eyes. And then the familiar scene.

At first, he thought he was back in his dream. There was Delaney, her mouth open in a silent scream. Everything was just like it was in the last transmutation of his nightmare: him standing to the side, watching in the blue light as his disembodied arms extended to her throat. He was puzzled by the moment. Why was he reliving the dream now after it had been dormant for so long? And why in his waking life?

He looked closer and realized something else was different. Her eyes were no longer aflame the way they'd always been before. They were simply the adorned, prosthetic eyes she wore now. He looked closer still at the neck and saw something even stranger.

His hands were old.

It didn't make sense. He looked down at his own hands. In the dim light of his vision he could see they were the same as always—slender and smooth, not the thicker, wrinkled hands that encircled Delaney's throat. He looked back and suddenly he knew.

Those aren't my hands.

He realized now that in every dream he had never looked at the source of those arms, those hands, too terrified of seeing himself in the act of killing the very person he'd wanted all along to save. He forced himself now to look.

Delaney's father—his face twisted by a horror that matched her own as she sank down at his feet—stood over her, his arms reaching out, his hands gripping her neck.

The image disappeared with another flash, and the darkness returned. Jacob realized he was gasping on the floor. He picked himself up and leaned against the wall, still reeling from the image.

It wasn't a dream. It was a vision like before.

He turned back and made his way down the hall, moving as silently as he could, hoping for any sound that might reveal where Delaney was. He had to warn her. He had to stop her and save her.

If only there were some light in here, he thought. He hated this darkness, hated trying to navigate without sight. He couldn't remember ever feeling so helpless back when he was blind. He thought of calling out to her but held back. He didn't want to wake the high councilor. If he was still asleep and Jacob could find Delaney, then maybe they could both get away before her father ever knew they were there. If her father was awake, Jacob didn't want to reveal himself until absolutely necessary.

Groping along, his hands came across an open doorway. He froze, leaning against the wall, and listened. Sure enough, he could hear the faint sound of snoring coming from the room. Delaney must be in there. What was she waiting for? *She must be nervous*, he thought. He didn't blame her—he was nervous too. He was about to leave the comfort of the doorway, strike out across the room to find her and get her out, when there was the rustling of sheets.

"Father?"

"Who is it?" the high councilor cried. Jacob started at the

voice. The man sounded feeble in his terror, so different from the man Jacob knew.

"It's me, Father. It's Delaney," she murmured.

The man didn't respond at first, but Jacob could hear his breathing, different now, fast and drawn.

"Delaney? Is it really you? How can this be?"

"I've come back."

"Back from where?" he asked. The fear disappeared from his voice, replaced with a familiar coldness. "From the Seers? You've been with them, haven't you. Did you bring them here? Does anyone else know you've returned?"

"No," she said. "I came to you first."

A long silence followed. Jacob could almost hear the high councilor thinking, processing the moment.

"Why have you come back?"

"I didn't like it out there," she said. "I knew I belonged here, with my own people."

There was a pause before the high councilor spoke. "You should have listened to me, Delaney. I warned you that the Seers would hurt you, that you would meet pain. Goodness knows how they've corrupted you."

"I'm glad I left Harmony, Father, even if it was just for a while," she said. Jacob could hear her own voice harden against the force of his, could hear her slipping into the rhythm of her old antagonism. But when she spoke again, her tone had softened. "You're right. There was pain, a lot of it. It was intense. But I've come back now, to stay. I want to be a part of the community again."

A minute passed. Jacob's heart began to pound as he waited for the man to reply. Why wasn't he responding?

"You can never come back to Harmony, Delaney," he said

232

at last, pausing to let the words sink in.

Jacob could feel her absorbing them, could feel them hanging in the darkness.

"For so many reasons you cannot come back. It would violate every principle of the Foundation. Who knows how many people you would infect, the kind of damage you would do. Harmony has already said good-bye to you. I've already said good-bye to you. It was a beautiful farewell, far greater than you deserved after your betrayal." He sounded weary. Weary and sad. Jacob heard him rise from the bed.

"Please, Father. You have to let me," she begged. "I'll tell people whatever you want me to about the Seers. And we can be a family again."

Jacob winced at her words. Suddenly, she was the Delaney he remembered from the very end of her days in Harmony—depressed, broken, and desperate.

"How?" her father exclaimed. "You're not the same anymore. You've been out there. You're not the daughter I once had. She's dead. In my mind, in everyone's mind, she no longer exists."

"Why did you have to tell them that?"

"I did it for their good, Delaney, and for yours."

The doorway suddenly filled with a light that spilled out into the hall. Jacob ducked back against the corridor wall. The blue light wasn't bright, but in the pitch-blackness of the house, it had its own intensity.

There could be only one reason for the light.

I was right all along, Jacob thought, seeing the high councilor wink all over again in his mind, the memory made more vivid by its confirmation. Delaney's father continued.

"A clean break is always—" His voice froze. The only

sound was the faintest hum of the light, like the quietest of sounders. "Your eyes!" he cried. "Look at what they did to you. What have you become?"

Jacob chanced a peek around the corner in time to see the man reaching, grabbing Delaney's arm so roughly that she cried out. She pulled away from him and collapsed on the bed, scuttling back until she cringed against the wall. Her eyes glittered in the light of the small lamp humming on a nearby table. The lamp, a cylinder of cold blue cased in steel, bathed the room more in shadows than in light. The gleam of her gold rims and diamond eyes disappeared as her father came forward to stand between her and the lamp, his back to Jacob.

Delaney couldn't see his shadow loom before her or the light that glowed behind him, but Jacob knew she didn't have to.

"The eyes don't work, not anymore. Not like yours, Father."

He sighed. "So now you know," he said. "The only one to ever find out."

A pang struck Jacob. *She's not the only one*, he thought. *I should have told her.*

"How long?" she asked.

"A long time. Since I was young. But not completely—it only came to one eye. But one was enough."

"Enough for what?"

"To have experienced all the sins of the Seers," he cried. The pain in his voice surprised Jacob. For a moment, he softened. He knew what that pain was like. "I succumbed to the same temptations, allowed myself to be tainted. I am a corruption, Delaney. Just like you, but in a different way." He paused. "So many times, I wanted to submit myself to the ghostbox, have my vision stripped away. More than once, I came close to cutting the eye out myself, like a secret Oedipus."

Jacob shuddered at the suggestion. The Oedipi—like his best friend Egan's father—were born as Seers but joined the Foundation and became Blinders by choice.

"But there's no grace in that sort of tragedy," the man continued. His voice began to shake as he sat down on the bed, took his daughter by the hand, and drew her to him. Jacob could see her tremble beneath her father's fingers that now traced the line of gold around her eyes, following the paths that receded across the temples and into her hair. "And I realized that my corruption had a purpose. It is the source of my moral authority. It allows me to realize daily why we need Harmony, why the Foundation is the truth. The people need me. I have tarnished myself for their sake—yet they must never know what I've done for them. That's the true tragedy, isn't it?"

He was now inches from her face and trembling as much as she. His fingers tightened along the sides of her head. Jacob watched in horror as she gripped the man's forearms, his dream unfolding as the man's hands moved down to her throat.

"What are you doing?" Jacob heard her gasp before the sound was squeezed off completely.

"I told you before that you were dead to me, Delaney," he said. "I have to do this, for all of us. I'm sorry."

He began repeating these last words, a consolation for them both as he wept and she gaped with open mouth.

Suddenly, he cried out, then stiffened, releasing his grip

235

as both of them collapsed onto the floor.

Jacob stood frozen over the two figures at his feet. The steel lamp in his hands, now filtered red with blood on one side, still glowed, unfazed by the blow. It was only Delaney's sudden gasp for air that stirred Jacob to movement. He dropped the light, which clattered and rolled, sending shadows dancing about the room, and rushed to her side. She continued gasping as he helped her sit up and cradled her in his arms.

"Are you okay?" he asked. She nodded, her mouth tightening in fear and sorrow, before breaking out into sobs. Her body shook as she cried, her hands instinctively raised to her eyes, though no tears could be shed.

"I think I killed him," Jacob whispered, looking at the red shadow against the floor.

A moment later there was a moan. The high councilor stirred beside them. Jacob forced himself to reach over and feel the man's head. A large welt had surfaced and blood matted the hair, but it wasn't as bad as Jacob had feared.

"Let's go," Delaney said. Jacob rose and helped her to her feet.

Though it had grown brighter outside, it was still early and the streets were quiet. They moved as quickly as possible, Delaney struggling to keep up with Jacob as he pulled her along behind him. Soon they worked out a rhythm and picked up the pace, disregarding the echo of their steps against the path. When they encountered people on the street, Jacob ignored the looks of confusion and fear that met the sound of their passing.

They approached the edge of town. Jacob felt a surge of relief at the sight of the cruiser parked on top of the ridge and

Xander in the distance, now running down the slope to meet them. Holding Delaney's hand, Jacob leaped into the tall grass. Xander, traveling much faster than the two of them could, caught up with them. Jacob could see the concern on his face as he noticed the bruises on Delaney's throat.

"We're all right," he reassured Xander in a loud whisper. They were all panting from the run.

"You have blood on you," Xander said, seeing Jacob's hands. Jacob looked down in surprise.

"I had to, Xander," he said in a choked voice. Now that he'd stopped moving, it had all begun to catch up with him. "Her father—he was hurting Delaney. He was trying to kill her."

"You did the right thing, Jacob. Now let's get out of here."

As he had the night of her rescue, Xander swept Delaney into his arms and headed across the meadow toward the hill where the cruiser waited. Jacob followed him at first, bounding to keep up with the man's long strides, before lagging behind. The adrenaline was fading and he felt tired, but he knew that wasn't the reason he was slowing down.

"Wait!" he shouted. Xander stopped and turned. "I have to go back."

"No. They might have found him by now. It isn't safe."

"I need to do what I came here to do. Please, Xander."

Xander sighed and put Delaney down. Pulling out his stunner, he walked to Jacob. He adjusted a few settings and tried handing the pistol to the boy, but Jacob refused it.

"I won't need it," he said. "Just go to the northern edge of the colony and wait."

"We'll be there," Delaney said, coming forward and taking Xander's hand.

Xander frowned briefly and shook his head. "Don't be long," he said, leading Delaney to the cruiser.

Jacob watched them as they climbed the hill together. "See you soon," he whispered back.

CHAPTER TWENTY

Jacob paused at the edge of the stone path leading to the distant bunker. Here the pathminders ended, and the squat shape rising out of the grass seemed detached, as if a piece of Harmony had broken off and was floating away. He looked around and, seeing no one nearby, headed out.

The last time he'd been here, in his dream, he'd been slow, fearful, following the high councilor's ghostly drift as the fire closed in behind them. Now he sped down the path, eager, light under the morning sky, until he reached the bunker.

Looking up as he approached, he half expected to see the enormous striped cat reclining across the top of the doorway as it had been in his dreams, but the spot was empty. To his surprise, Jacob felt a moment of disappointment—he wouldn't have minded the comfort of a familiar face right now, even that of an animal's.

A small panel to the right of the door contained a narrow slot. He walked over to the panel, reached up, and inserted the card Delaney had given him into the slot. There was a loud, metallic click and the great door slid open with a hiss.

Jacob took a deep breath and stepped into the darkness.

As before, both in real life and in his dream, the ghostbox

chamber was cool and quiet, a murky room of ambient light. As he entered, the monolith at the center of the room waited, its one dark eye glowing suddenly to life.

Jacob hesitated. What was one supposed to say to a machine?

"Good morning," he said, at last, deciding at least to be polite.

"Good morning," the voice said, startling Jacob. It spoke in the same timbre from his dream: an androgynous voice, calm, knowing, servile.

"You *do* speak," Jacob whispered.

A beam from the solitary yellow eye shot forth and washed over him, scanning every inch of his body.

"You are not High Councilor Martin Corrow," the ghostbox said.

"No, I'm not," Jacob replied. "Do you know who I am?"

"You are Jacob Manford."

"Do you know why I'm here?"

"I do not know," the ghostbox replied in a matter-of-fact tone. "You were scheduled for termination, but it did not occur."

Jacob shivered, remembering once again the high councilor's final words before Jacob had torn himself away. *Let's just hope the surgery goes well, Jacob. The ghostbox makes mistakes from time to time.*

"By whose order?"

"High Councilor Martin Corrow, under instruction from the Foundation. By the Foundation's order, all abominations are to be terminated."

Jacob had done his final report for civics class on the Foundation. He knew that even the high councilor had to answer to the orders it gave from its headquarters on Earth. But abomination? Jacob wondered what that meant.

"What's an abomination?"

"According to Foundation policy, all those who have acquired the sight mutation are to be treated as abominations."

"Mutation," Jacob said, repeating the word to himself. Was that a good or bad thing? It didn't sound good. "Is that what I have?" he asked the ghostbox.

"Yes."

"Are there others who have it too?"

"Yes."

Jacob paused and took a deep breath. *Now for the most important question.*

"Where are they? What happened to all of them?"

There was a momentary silence. "Please wait while I search my files," the ghostbox replied. The sound of distant voices came in through the open door. Jacob ran to the entrance and peeked out. A group of men had just entered the path leading to the ghostbox. They were Listeners, men who policed the colony, making sure everyone followed the rules.

How did they know to come here? he wondered. Had he been discovered?

As they drew closer, Jacob noticed some of them carried finders. He glanced down at the high councilor's key still in his hand. Could they be programmed to zero in on it? He shook his head and pulled back inside.

"Well?" he cried, staring up at the glowing monocle.

"One moment," it purred.

Hurry up! Jacob wanted to scream. The men were getting closer. He wasn't worried about confronting the Listeners outside, but he didn't want to be stuck in a room with them or, worse, be sealed inside and at their mercy.

"There are no known locations for those you have requested," the ghostbox intoned. Jacob felt his stomach sink. "However," it added, "Foundation records show a suspected group of abominations are believed to have gathered on Teiresias, though confirmation is pending. I shall now produce the reports in full."

"That's okay," Jacob replied. "But thanks anyway."

He placed the high councilor's key on the floor and dashed for the exit as the ghostbox began reciting.

Plunging through the doorway, Jacob pulled up at the sight of the Listeners only ten yards away. Hearing him, they started as well, slipping into a crouch as they raised what Jacob suddenly realized were pistols. They were different than the stunner Xander had offered him, larger, with barrels that widened into cones. He dodged sideways, running as fast as he could. From the corner of his eye he could see a wave of distortion roll toward the bunker doorway, as if the air between them was melting, and he leaped, feeling the wall of energy roll past him, brushing his back, its force propelling him forward into the grass.

Recovering, he tore off through the field, turning in a wide arc back toward the colony, where he could weave his way north through the maze of streets in safety. He took one last look behind him at the bunker before disappearing around the corner. The Listeners were following, but they were no longer a threat. He turned and headed for the northern edge of the colony where Xander and Delaney waited.

Coming into the North Tier Square, Jacob stopped for a moment to rest. He splashed his hands into the fountain, washing off the dried blood. The water felt cool, and when his hands were clean, he took a long drink.

Several people walked in the square. He watched as they passed in and out. No matter how many times he had witnessed this scene, it still made him anxious to be unknown in the midst of other people. His entire trip through the colony had only intensified this feeling. Watching the figures drift along the streets among the dirty concrete buildings and pitted walkways made him feel like a ghost come back to haunt the scene of his crime. Sometimes it seemed as if they were ghosts and that he was the only person alive. Either way, Harmony was different now because he had changed, and it satisfied him to realize that nothing here would be missed. Except for one thing.

He glanced back from where he'd come. There was no sign he'd been followed.

There's enough time, he thought. He could spare a moment to say good-bye.

The street was empty as he made his way to his former home, pausing as he neared the steps. The door was open to let in the morning air. He slipped silently to the threshold and looked in.

His mother sat quietly before an empty place at the table. There was no sign of his father. It was so much like his dreams, for a moment he looked back, half expecting to see the color drain from the street, smell the burning in the air as the flowers withered to ash.

His mother sat motionless but for the movement of her hands, which turned a small silver cube over and over, stopping occasionally to caress its textured sides. It was Jacob's music box, the one she'd given him weeks ago for his birthday. She opened the lid and the familiar tune began to issue forth, the tiny notes evenly plinking their simple song. He continued to watch her as the tune ended and after the briefest pause repeated itself again. She was singing with it now, first humming the melody then mouthing the words in a husky whisper, her tender voice sounding more fragile than the tiny machine.

Finally she closed the lid and set the box on the table at the place where he used to sit. He opened his mouth to greet her, but she suddenly rose from the table. She went over to the piano, sat down, and began playing. It was a new song, one Jacob had never heard her play before. As the song grew louder, the notes pounding around the house, another noise from behind him made him turn. Again, as at the ghostbox, he could hear the distant shouts of men. *They must be searching the whole community*, he thought. Or maybe they had discovered the intruder's identity and guessed where he would most likely have gone. He couldn't stay.

He turned back to where his mother still played, lost in the tune. He couldn't interrupt her now—there would be no time to say the things he wanted to say. Worse, if he was discovered, it could mean trouble for her.

Glancing down, he caught sight of a nearby flowerbed. He spotted some yellow flowers, ones with a black center, and plucked five from their bed, ducking inside and laying them on the table by his music box as the voices outside grew closer.

Leaving the house, he crossed the street and climbed up the grassy slope of the other side, peering down from the neighbor's roof as the Listeners entered the lane. As they rushed toward his house, he remembered the last time he'd escaped Harmony. *It's just like before*, he thought, turning away. But as he came back into the square, he realized it wasn't. Before he was running away, frightened and alone. Now there were people who waited, eager for his return. He took one last look at the fountain and left the square.

After that, he didn't stop. He only ran, back to the edge of the northern tier, over the top, and down the hill into the fields where he and Egan had often raced, where he had run that day he first left Harmony in fear. He was breathing hard, but he didn't care. He didn't stop running. He didn't even hear the wail of the pathminders when he burst across the colony perimeter. He just focused his sight on the distant point where Xander's cruiser waited on the horizon.

EPILOGUE

There we are, he thought.

Jacob was flying, soaring over the plain like one of the falcons that inhabited the open skies. Spotting the figures on the crest, walking together through the grass, he began dropping toward the land, swooping in for a better look.

As he drew closer something puzzled him. Usually in this particular dream it was the three of them, with Delaney in the center, her white gown flowing, escorted by Xander and himself. But as he swept overhead, he saw that there were only two. He was missing.

Sailing by, he chalked it up to the distortion of his dreams. Though he had grown used to the lucid visions that marked most nights' passage, he was always startled by the little ways the details changed, how the permutations of his mind gave reality its subtle twists.

Gliding to a landing, he turned toward the pair in the distance and waited eagerly for them to approach, his shadow stretched before him, long against the setting sun that had painted the sky gold. He gasped in wonder as Duna, swiftly cresting the horizon behind them, silhouetted the approaching figures. They continued to draw nearer and still Jacob wondered why he wasn't with the pair. Then they were running and laughing, bounding toward him through the grass, Xander leading Delaney by the hand and waving, as if in greeting.

How do they see me? Jacob wondered. In his dreams, he was always invisible, a watcher without form.

Jacob heard a rustle in the grass behind him and turned in time to see himself hurrying to meet them, dropping a worn pack and breaking into a run. *So I am here, after all,* he thought. But something was different. He drew a sharp breath at the sight of the older features on his young man's face and at the taller body, broad shouldered, sure of himself. There was something in the run, in its urgency and its confidence, that told him he'd been gone, had traveled great distances only to come back once again.

He drew up and watched, unable to contain his own smile, as the young man met the pair, joining them in a group embrace before turning back to the moonrise, the three of them arm in arm.

A moment later he was back in the air, watching the linked figures shrink against the plain below as he raced toward the glittering rings of Duna.

Jacob was still soaring when he woke. The feeling of lightness followed him as he dressed and descended the stairs for breakfast. Xander and Delaney were at the table, talking, laughing. Nine months had passed since their trip to Harmony, and the bruises on Delaney's neck had long since healed. Watching the two of them, Jacob wondered if Delaney could sense the smile on Xander's face as he gazed at her.

"Morning," Jacob said, coming to the table.

"Good morning, sleepy," Delaney said. "I was wondering if you were ever going to wake up."

"He must have been having a good dream," Xander joked.

"You could say that," Jacob said.

"I'm heading out for a drive," Xander told him. "Hurry up and eat some breakfast if you want to come."

"Just make sure you're back by lunchtime," Delaney broke in. "You promised to read to me this afternoon, didn't you, Jacob?"

"I did," Jacob replied. Xander was still teaching him every day, using the first book Kala had given him, though she'd given him others since.

"Don't worry, we'll be back in time. Won't we, Jacob?"

Jacob looked at the two of them at the table and smiled. "Everything'll be fine," he said. He sat down at the table between them and closed his eyelids, the dream still heavy upon him. He was still flying in his mind's eye, but by now he'd left the atmosphere, had passed Duna and the sun and had headed out for deeper space, drawn by a force he couldn't resist and didn't want to. And suddenly he knew. The months of waiting were over. Now was the time.

"Xander," he said, opening his eyes. "Tell me about Teiresias."